What Educators and Community Advocates say about the Mission Bells Trilogy

Twisted Cross, Book I

"Throughout the book, Sal struggles with his impulses toward corruption, but key relationships he makes along the way often steer his actions away from mischief. But not always. *Twisted Cross* weaves together historical figures and events with a sobering frankness that transports readers to an era too often romanticized."

—Claudia Armann, author

"Salvador, a lusty youngster, learns about the world quickly. The female characters are vividly drawn, especially Rosa in Mazatlán. The monks are not to be trusted, especially the Bishop, who fears the Natives and wants to destroy their history, yet, Brother David, becomes an important figure in Sal's life."

—Dr. Geoff Aggeler, award-winning novelist,
biographer, critic and veteran writing teacher

"This is a fast-paced novel, book 1 of the *Mission Bells Trilogy*, that would keep a high school student reading. There are young adult discussion themes throughout the book. Friendship, betrayal by community and family members, and the desire for adventure and wealth are just a few that could be amplified by a good teacher. There are several references to actual historic persons and events throughout the novel. This could be used in an English or Social Studies setting. The author offers a Reader's Guide to assist teachers and readers."

—S. M. Heacock, retired Los Angeles
Unified School District Administrator

"This isn't just for kids! Really nice job for a first-time novelist! Blending characters and history on an exciting, compelling and realistic journey to become a good man and overcome the challenges that all kids face making the right choices in life."

—Anonymous

"I started reading this book and couldn't put it down! The story of Sal's adventures provides an unvarnished picture of a boy growing into manhood, along with all the family dysfunctions and youthful temptations that have potential to turn him away from fulfilling his destiny. What I appreciated was the way Sal's life is told in the context of Spain and the New World, which opens a window into the personal experiences of 'regular' people of this time period. I recommend this book for anyone who would like an exciting, fast-paced adventure that shows the internal and external struggles of a young man learning to become a person of character."

—P. Wiggins, community foundations

Golden Secrets, Book II

"As a lover of history, I enjoyed reading the story and am curious about where the next book will take the readers. I appreciate that the story brought out events and life scenes that are not normally experienced in history books of this period. It's an accurate depiction of the role of women, demeaned and objectified. The dynamics with the Native people are also on par with what was happening at that time."

—J. Parrish, educator

"Alicia has passion and is appalled by injustice, but still open to learning. She is thrown into situations beyond her abilities and tries to solve problems using the skills she has, motivated by a love for family and friends.

The emotions between characters were really strong as Alicia realizes she is losing Nina while also bonding with Clara. There are still strong differences in the way the sisters see the world, but they are sharing secrets and collaborating on plans for the family."

—C. Degelman, educator

"I liked seeing Alicia's transition from a tomboy to a young woman. She was courageous, tenacious and clever and had her own thoughts. Seeing her grow into herself was a great story."

—P. Wiggins, community foundations

"Padre Romo was my favorite character because he was steady, understanding, open, intuitive and human. He was able to give an overview of the history and events that preceded the story. He seems to be involved and know how to handle most of the calamities and personalities."

—P. Sweeney, retired educator

Golden Secrets

MISSION BELLS 2 OF 3

ANITA PEREZ FERGUSON

GOLDEN SECRETS
Copyright © 2021 Anita Perez Ferguson

Published by Luz Publications
P.O. Box 90651
Santa Barbara, CA 93190

Design and Distribution by Bublish, Inc.

ISBN 978-0-9673300-4-4 (paperback)
ISBN: 978-0-9673300-6-8 (eBook)

Publisher's Cataloging-In-Publication Data
(Prepared by The Donohue Group, Inc.)

Names: Perez Ferguson, Anita, author.
Title: Golden secrets / Anita Perez Ferguson.
Description: Santa Barbara, CA : Luz Publications, [2021] | Series:
Mission bells ; 2 of 3 | In English with occasional Spanish. | Title
from cover. | Interest age level: 016-024. | Summary: "Golden Secrets
features the lives of young Mexican, Spanish and indigenous California
girls who are aggressively courted by land-hungry Yankees and rough-
cut fur traders in the Spanish colony"—Provided by publisher.

Identifiers: ISBN 9780967330044 (paperback)
| ISBN 9780967330068 (ebook)

Subjects: LCSH: Teenage girls—California—History—18th century—
Fiction. | Hispanic American girls—California—History—18th century—
Fiction. | Colonists—California—History—18th century—Fiction. |
Courtship—California—History—18th century—Fiction. | California—
Colonization—History—18th century—Fiction. | Young adult fiction.
| LCGFT: Historical fiction. Classification: LCC PS3616.E743 G65
2021 (print) | LCC PS3616.E743 (ebook) | DDC 813/.6 [Fic]—dc23

Dedication

To my father and mother,
William Macias Perez (1919–1987) and
Ortencia Teresa Gonzales Perez (1919–1998),
Native Californians who raised three
daughters in a loving home,

and to my husband,
G. William Ferguson V,
who I had the good fortune to marry in 1972.

Finally, to the original inhabitants of our coastal homeland,
the Chumash people,
I pay my respects to their elders, past, present, and future.

𝔄 Timeline

1400   Evidence appears of Indigenous peoples inhabiting the Pacific coastline in organized fishing and trading communities.

1515   Three hundred years of Spanish colonization begins in Central America and portions of South America.

1769   Franciscan missionaries begin to establish the missions in Alta California under Spanish rule.

1782   The Spanish Martinez expedition explores the northern Pacific coast.

1815   Mexico gains independence from Spain and resumes territorial control, including control of Alta California.

1829   Shipwrecks of Spanish trading vessels along the central Alta California territory include the Dorotea in 1829, the Fama in 1846, and the Reliance in 1878.

1830   **Our story begins . . .**

Alicia Ortega faces these challenges and more

01

Chapter

The *hacienda* stood above the *Refugio* harbor on the site of an old Spanish lookout post. The building bricks and roof tiles were crafted by local Natives, who witnessed sunken ships, golden treasures, and many a sailor scattered along the Pacific shores in the 1800s. Alicia Ortega lived in that hacienda; today she wore Mama's faded apron and dusted the family altar, praying to Mother Mary, a ceramic saint.

"Help guard our home while Mama and Papa are gone and forgive me for sneaking into my sister's diary."

"*Cuidate, mija,*" Mother Mary said. Alicia backed away from the statue, not wanting to hear the warnings.

A *Chumash* worker, Nina, swept ashes from the hearth. The Ortega family needed household help in the dusty *adobe*. Alicia and Nina were close. Some days they pretended they were sisters.

Alicia was just fourteen years old. She lived with her real sisters, Dolores, the eldest, and Clara, the middle sister; and with their mother and father in the hacienda on the cliff above the Refugio harbor. Then things changed.

"What did Dolores leave behind?" Alicia and Nina scrambled up the stairs to a sleeping loft, a small dim space above the family *sala*. The loft had a bed, a window, and a few pegs on the wall. Nina stooped to collect laundry in Dolores's abandoned room.

"Find rags. Two moons, no rags." Nina lay flat to reach around the sleeping crates, her black braid speckled with lint. Dressed in a stained apron made from a muslin flour sack, she spoke some Spanish, learned from the Franciscans.

"Look." Nina held up a small envelope with handwriting on the flap. "To my sisters." Alicia snatched the envelope and read the note inside.

> Dear Sisters,
>
> I am on the way to the Laredo School for Young Ladies. Imagine that: I am now a young lady. I am excited to travel and enroll with the finest girls from the best *familias* in all the northern territories.
>
> Mama and Papa insisted on coming. I apologize for taking them from you. They were in such a hurry to see me off to school. I cannot imagine why. Clara, you can take over my sleeping loft. Alicia, someday you will understand why older girls need privacy. Nina, take good care of my sisters.
>
> I said my goodbyes to dear Captain Harris—my sailor with the ocean blue eyes. Someday soon I will be Mrs. Harris. Also, I gave my confession to *Padre* Romo to prepare

for this journey. Write to me when your spelling improves. I may be too busy to respond but will remember you in my prayers.

Your sister, Dolores

Alicia tossed the letter aside and continued her search of the loft.

"Why are we looking for more rags?"

"Girl make blood—use rags. No rags—girl make baby," Nina mumbled as she searched under the bed and in the clothes hamper.

"But you said Dolores didn't dirty rags for two months. Two moons, I remember." Alicia thrashed through the bedsheets. "What's that mean?"

"Dolores make captain's baby," Nina said. Alicia's face grew hot with the revelation.

02

Chapter

licia slumped to the floor and crossed her legs in front of her. She was shaken by the news of how and why girls bled and the revelation that her sister Dolores was pregnant. She thought back over the events of the previous days.

After Alicia reported the secrets of her sister's diary to Mama, her parents rushed to enroll Dolores in the Laredo School for Young Ladies. No one talked about the Ortega sisters ever going away to school before the diary incident. Alicia repeated a line from the diary to herself. "I lay below and gaze up at Harris, my sailor with his ocean blue eyes." Now the passionate entries discovered in Dolores's journal made more sense.

Nina tugged on Alicia's curls. "You sick? We work now," she said.

"I can't. Why didn't anyone tell me why Dolores was leaving?" Alicia looked around the loft and recalled the days when she looked up to her sisters, even though she never truly felt she understood them.

"Dolores ready to be mama," Nina said. "No worry."

"But Captain Harris? Why pick him? You remember how we snuck peeks at her other boyfriends when we were little?"

"She always like boys. I remember," Nina grinned and sat on the floor next to Alicia. When the two of them started these remembering times it always took a while to finish.

"You're right. She was always eager to meet the boys. Remember when she was caught trying to hold that boy's hand, the young novitiate, Brother Timothy?"

"He left quick, to another mission." Nina felt like part of the family when she shared such memories.

"After that it was Emilio, the clerk who made deliveries to our house once a month." Alicia looked toward Nina, "Did you live here then?"

"*Cierto*, I remember."

"Then, Captain Harris, at Papa's dock—and right away she told Mama she was sure God intended her to give herself over to him."

"She did. I saw them lying on a canvas in a dinghy," Nina said.

"You did? Why didn't you tell me?"

"She made me promise. Said it was her holy service. Your papa was mad, so I keep quiet," Nina said. "Your papa say bad things. 'Jesus, Mary and Joseph,' he said."

"Well, now we know the whole story. Dolores is going to this Laredo school."

"With Captain Harris's baby in her belly." Nina tugged on Alicia's arm. "We work now."

Alicia might not understand everything the grownups did, but she intended to guard the family home while her parents were away with Dolores.

03

Chapter

On the same day that Mama and Papa took Dolores away, Captain Harris and other grubby buccaneers off-loaded black-market goods at Papa's dock, Refugio.

"No taxes here, mates, and the bonus is that the harbor master has three daughters! This place is a gold mine." Harris hummed to himself, straightening his tattered coat and turning to the hacienda on the bluff.

Safe from the Spanish harbor taxes of 1805, the wharf was not truly a secret to anyone. Even some of the Mission padres used the dock to bargain for linens, silks, and ornaments.

"Finish unloading the merchandise while I patrol up the hill and inspect Papa's little treasures." Captain Harris reached the *veranda* steps at the hacienda and announced, "I can help Clara run the dock if you let me." He slid his muddy boot close to wedge the door open. Too close.

Alicia saw him approach and leaned against the other side of the door. She and Harris were only inches apart and she studied his face.

"You should not be here," Alicia cried out. "Dolores is not here. Mama and Papa are gone too." No one entered the house when her parents were away, especially not sailors.

Nina helped defend the house by shaking a dust mop through the door's opening. She shooed Harris from the patio with the *manzanita* branch, pine needles glued with pitch to the end. "You go now."

"Why?" Harris laughed. He knew his business at Papa's black-market port was safe. His ragtag crew were only a step above common pirates, but they could slip past the customs officers stationed at the *Presidio*. The distance of Papa's place from the official custom's collectors made it popular as a tax-free landing for *savvy* traders like Captain Harris.

Alicia leaned with all her might against the door. Harris continued to push against the entry like it was some kind of game. He offered Alicia a sly smile. She looked him over. He could be handsome when he washed and shaved, which was seldom. Today he wore ragged dungarees, a patched jacket and a knit cap tugged down over a sunburned face and straggly hair, looking like all the other ruffians. Except for those piercing blue eyes. Something about them signaled that his family was not from Alta California. His expression, full of greed, held Alicia's attention for a moment.

04

Chapter

Clara slept late, but the commotion at the front door with Captain Harris woke her up. Clara found the cast-off letter from Dolores and rushed down to the *sala*.

"You know," she said, "I'm taking over Dolores's things. It's all mine now." She stood behind Alicia, hands planted on her hips, in a taffeta skirt and a lacy blouse, instead of the work clothes she usually wore for a day at home. Clara wrapped herself in one of Dolores's old shawls and swished the fringe in Nina's face.

"Did you iron my dress like I asked, you lazy girl?" she said to Nina. "I am going to the *fiesta* at the Mission. Captain Charles Harris invited me." She said it loudly, so that Harris heard her and stopped pushing on the door. Alicia hated to see Nina bossed around by Clara, who obviously wanted to take charge of the *rancho* while Mama and Papa were gone. Clara always got her way; attending the Mission fiesta with Captain Harris would be no exception.

"But you can't; he is Dolores's fiancé! I know things." Alicia stepped back from the door. Did others know why Mama and Papa took her sister away?

"You think you are the only one who knows about our careless big sister? No wonder she wanted her privacy in that sleeping loft." Clara waved out the door, chattering to Captain Harris.

"Let's do something before she starts more trouble." Alicia searched Nina's expression to see if she understood what was going on. "It's up to us to protect Rancho Refugio." One sister had already given in to Harris. Alicia would not let him ruin the whole family, but how could she stop him? She watched Clara slip out the front door to flirt with the captain.

Alicia peered through the window at her sister and the captain. Nina peeked over her shoulder.

"Did I ever tell you about first time Clara shamed the family? It was in the church."

"With the padres?" Nina wanted to hear more.

"She was only nine. I was seven. Clara resisted taking her First Communion at the Mission." Alicia remembered the event as if it was yesterday.

"That big sin, a bad thing," Nina knew the Mission rules.

"Not on *my* tongue!" Clara had screamed, right there in the service, when Padre Romo offered communion.

"What happened? Punishment?" Nina had suffered her share of Mission punishments for much lesser crimes.

"Papa's big donations to the Mission helped. The padre excused her after she made such a fuss. She always gets her way." Her sister was bossy, so Alicia usually kept her distance, but this time the stakes were too high. Alicia knew what Harris had done to Dolores. He must have known that the first of the Ortega sisters to marry would receive a huge land grant in her dowry. Now he was going to try his luck with Clara.

05

Chapter

The days after the Mission fiesta, *pueblo* folks gossiped about the Ortega family. Once Harris and Clara made a public display, more neighbors took the long walk to come by the hacienda. They stopped to drop bread or milk in exchange for a bit of gossip.

"Aren't you proud of your popular sisters?" they said. Alicia tried to ignore such embarrassing questions about Clara dancing with her sister's fiancé. "You must miss your mama and papa. There is so much work to be done here. How long will they stay away?"

Clara grew angry when she heard the townsfolk's nosy comments.

"Our mama said she was our age when she built this rancho with Papa and his brothers. And she even had a baby. We will be just fine, thank you very much," Clara said.

After the gossip died down, Harris started to visit the Ortega garden as if he expected to become the master of the house. He spread muddy footprints everywhere he tromped.

Alicia monitored these visits from the shade of the cooking *ramada*, a thatched awning that kept the noonday sun from ruining the food, where she and Nina shelled peas and ground corn on a *molcajete*. A wooden plank and a few buckets under the ramada made up the space they used for food preparation.

Harris prowled the grounds, taking notice of every detail of the hacienda. He examined the trumpet vine winding its way around the arbor and picked up a lemon fallen from the tree. On one visit Alicia thought she heard him exhale, "At last."

What did he mean, "at last?" Had he mumbled on, musing that at last he could corner the second Ortega sister alone? Did he think he found access to their property? Maybe he planned to trick a silly girl whose papa controlled a land grant into marriage to gain a gift of property from her dowry.

"A perfect day for a perfect young lady." Harris greeted Clara on that visit with an exaggerated bow. Her giggles floated across the garden. "None of these flowers can compete with your beauty."

"Welcome back to Rancho Refugio, Captain. It seems we are the talk of the pueblo." Clara dipped her chin and pinched her cheeks to make them rosy. Was she lovestruck by Harris?

"I am embarrassed by your attentions," Clara went on, leaning against the garden shed. Was she impressed by his charm? Alicia determined that this pesky man only pretended to love Clara. "Your adventures are so thrilling. Tell me more about your plans, Captain."

Harris must have thought Clara would be the sister to fulfill his land-hungry desires. He already tried her older sister Dolores, but she disappeared to Laredo after they got serious and spoke of marriage.

Then Alicia heard Harris say the same thing to Clara that she'd read in Dolores's diary.

"We will surprise your papa with a quick marriage, my dear. Trust me, I know the law. This land is your rightful dowry."

Would he trick Clara into plotting against the family? He was a man; Clara was her older sister. But Alicia needed to figure out some way to stop them.

06

Chapter

Alicia didn't plan to use magic to solve her problems at first, but by the time Nina suggested a visit to her grandmother, Alicia was desperate for any kind of help she could get. Alicia knew the old woman was a healer for the original tribe that lived on the Mission lands.

"Big trouble, Masagawa help." Nina shared her plan. "We go village, see Masagawa." Nina's grandmother had the strangest name.

"I know you want to help, but this is serious business. How can your grandma's magical cures help?" Alicia resisted the idea at first. Plus, she remembered her mother's warnings about Nina's tribal village; she said it had dark magic. Nina's grandmother and brothers clung to the old ways.

Then again, Alicia envied Nina's skills and confidence, her ability to see how Harris brought trouble to the house. She seemed to possess the knowledge of a grown woman. How could they be the same age? After all, Nina was just their household helper. The title to the rancho was at stake, and Alicia needed official help.

"Remember, we get good medicine for your Mama?" Nina referred to the times when they were younger. Alicia and Nina once hid healing tokens around the Ortega house for minor problems—for good spirits and protection. Masagawa's herbal mixtures often found a way into Mama's teas, stews, and even Papa's liquor bottles.

"Good for cough," Nina once instructed Alicia. "This one for courage, this to bring sleep." On many past occasions Nina secretly sprinkled, stirred, and sometimes splashed magic potions over the Ortega family home. Mama never tasted the special healing herbs.

Now Alicia faced big troubles, including the threat to Papa's land grant. She needed more than magic to protect the Ortega family from the scoundrel Harris. Out of respect for Masagawa she would go to the village, but afterward she would find another adult to help.

"I'll go to the village, but promise never to tell Mama." It was up to Alicia to stop Harris and his cheating schemes.

The following day, after they completed the household chores, the girls left the hacienda. Nina knew every trail leading away from the hacienda. On one side a pathway lead toward the dock and sloped downward in a sandy trail. In another direction, past the old cabin, tangled reeds hung over the twisting Mission trail.

They walked along a third path, hidden from view, a patch of stony ground that led upward toward Nina's tribal village. Before they left the house they exchanged their aprons and wore a cloth satchel slung over their shoulders. Both Mama and Masagawa had trained them to collect berries, special herbs, stones, and shells they found along the pathways. Some were said to have magical powers, if prepared just right.

07

Chapter

It was an hour's walk to the village, with many distractions along the way. Nina seemed to have a lot on her mind.

"My turn for remember game, okay with you?" Nina always listened to Alicia's memories. This was the first time the roles were reversed. Alicia thought she knew all about Nina already, but as the girls neared the village, Nina talked about her prior life among her own people.

Masagawa was the closest kin Nina had, not counting her two brothers. Her father died working as a scout for the *Portolá* expedition. It was up to Nina to care for her grandma, Masagawa, as she got older. This responsibility numbered her days with Alicia. Nina shared stories, all of them new to Alicia.

"Mama die when I come." Nina twisted a long strand of grass in her hands, biting off one end. "She leave Nina brothers." She picked up two loose stones and tossed them against a tree trunk. "Grandma take me. Masagawa carry me and feed me sweet berries and honey. When I grow and stand, she give sage bundle and songs." When Nina spoke of her grandmother, she smiled. She bent to pick up the tiniest frog and place it in the stream.

"Later, I learn her magic, special chants. I thought Masagawa my mama; brothers tell me no, when I make five years." Alicia wanted to reach out and touch her, but she just listened to her talk.

"We fight many times. Brothers blamed me when Mama die. They tell me she left me to work for them." Alicia thought it was a horrid thing for Nina's brothers to do. She was glad she had no brothers.

"At six years, White men take us to the Mission school. Grandma try to stop them. She tell me no forget sage songs. She say someday I sing for people." Nina waved her hand over her head pretending to hold the sage.

"Many children in school, talk other words. Padres say, you all talk Spanish." Alicia realized she never tried to learn any words in Nina's language.

"After Spanish words, I make broom from branch and pine needles. Like broom at Mama's altar." Alicia pictured the broom.

"We do laundry for the padres. Wash like Masagawa, clothes in the stream and rubbed with rock and jute root. Later, they send me to you, Alicia, and family."

Alicia did not make a response. Did this happen to all Native children? Mama taught her that the Mission made Native lives better and rescued them from their heathen ways. She said the family gave Nina a civilized life.

08

Chapter

"We home." Nina was now in charge. The entire Native village spread across the meadow behind the Mission. "Masagawa powerful healer, some Catholic visit for cures. They suffer long time."

These were Alicia's initial steps into Nina's territory, the sounds and smells unlike those at home. Wide-eyed, she entered the encampment and without thinking, she made the sign of the cross on her forehead. She saw children with jet black hair, like Nina's, playing and laughing together. They tossed white seashells in a flat basket and created a little rhythm. Women, draped with beaded necklaces, knelt low, at work over cooking fires. Everyone seemed much happier than the Native workers at the Mission.

The men pounded wooden tools and crafted handheld hunting weapons. Alicia tried to look away because they wore only narrow belts around their bare hips. Compared to Papa and her uncles, who had enormous bellies and balding heads, these men had lean bodies and dark, long hair. They were talkative, not frightening, lazy, or savage as others warned.

This world hidden from White settlers, not the Ortega family's rancho, was Nina's true home. That thought disturbed Alicia. The women looked up and smiled as the girls entered Grandma Masagawa's small hut, a dome of twigs tied together with long grasses.

"You sit here," Nina said. "Friend." Nina introduced her to a mound of dark cloth seated on a jute mat. Alicia squinted to see Masagawa's face. The old woman stretched out her hand. A sweet smoky smell hung in the air. A dim light entered through a gap in the reeds overhead. Grandma, wrinkled and trembling with palsy, held her palm up and waved it in Alicia's face.

"She make blessing on Dolores," Nina said.

"How does she know?" Alicia saw Masagawa had coal-black eyes folded deep in her leathery face. The old woman, humming, reached forward to smooth the sand floor. "What is she doing?"

"You watch, I go." Nina moved out of the hut. Alicia watched the old woman moving a reed bundle, tied to look like a little person. Masagawa drew a circle around the doll with her finger in the dirt and placed a small seashell next to it.

Waving her hand, Masagawa said, "Baba." Did this represent a blessing for Dolores and her new baby? It was an odd prayer. Should Alicia hold her hands together and bow her head, the only praying she knew? She could not keep herself from thinking about who might help her get rid of Harris. Masagawa held out the little shell and pressed it into Alicia's hand, closing her fingers around it.

"Baba." Did Masagawa hear Alicia's prayers? Was "baba" an answer to her questions? The morning lingered while they waited for Nina to return. The women bent over the doll in silence in the hot, stuffy hut. All that kept Alicia from dozing off was Grandma Masagawa's wheeze. Each breath had a hum and a quick whistle.

Angry voices rose just outside the hut. Nina's brothers? That thought startled Alicia. She wished the old woman was awake. She recalled her papa's disapproval of the brothers, locked up in the Presidio for drunkenness, so different from Nina. She hoped to avoid them, but it was too late now.

"We go." Nina pushed into her grandma's hut. Masagawa's eyes opened. "Go now!" She tugged on Alicia's arm.

"I'm coming, uh, goodbye." Alicia stooped through the hut's doorway and went out into the commotion. Nina stood outside, the object of her brothers' taunts and threats.

The brothers had Native names, but the padre insisted on calling them *Pedro* and *Flaco*. When Alicia was young, they worked at Rancho Refugio and the padre gave them a conditional reference. "They are strong, but often tempted to help themselves to extra tools. They yield to temptation and get in trouble."

"Work done—we take." The brothers determined the tools were theirs, since they were rarely paid for their labor. Each year the villagers lost hunting land, their freedom, and their women, who were sequestered making blankets and baskets for others. Now the brothers made their living as guides to Yankee trappers and Russian hunters.

Nina stood next to a White man wearing leather leggings and a rabbit fur cap. She tried to get Alicia's attention.

"Who is that White man?" Alicia asked. He was outfitted like a trapper, not like anyone who lived in the pueblo. Nina's brothers, one short, one skinny, pointed to the big fellow's weapons. The scrawny brother, Flaco, wore a leather strap across his chest. It held a pouch of arrows and a fishing spear.

"Sister must obey family." The skinny brother drew out a blade, threatening Nina. Alicia watched the other brother use a flat, smooth stone from his belt to sharpen his spear. He pretended to give his weapon all his attention but she knew he was aware of her gaze.

"Let's finish this business." The White trapper laid down his rifle. He withdrew a short broad knife from a leather sheath, wiped it on his pant leg, and placed it before Pedro. The brothers picked up the weapons and admired them.

"Good trade. Now go, Nina!" They jutted out their chins toward the White man. Their sneers revealed their worn-down brown teeth.

"Now, my Nina." The trapper grinned and nodded to Nina, looking her up and down. He waved her forward, on a pathway that led away from the village.

"Brothers trade me." Nina walked away. She did not look back, and no one helped her.

"Brothers what? You mean, exchange? They can't trade their sister." Nina took the wrong pathway. "Why are we going this way? Does he mean to follow us?" Alicia could hear the panic rising in her own voice. She clutched the seashell, hoping it held good magic.

"Humph." The trapper made a snorting noise. He raised his rugged walking staff. "You show me now."

"Brothers trade me for gun and knife. Now I show man secret Mission gate." Nina looked straight ahead. The girls took extra steps to keep ahead of the trapper. They caught their breath when he paused to listen to a bird's whistle or place his fingers on an animal print in the sand.

"Why show him the gate? What does he want?" Alicia, eager to return to the hacienda, said, "Just remember, you work for our family, not for this filthy trapper."

"Nina do what brothers say, ask no questions." Nina pulled away from Alicia. She walked ahead. "Gate for slop buckets—stinks." Her voice was so faint Alicia misheard her.

Alicia heard, "You stink." That was enough to keep her quiet. What did this man want at the Mission? Did Nina know the answer?

09

Chapter

After Nina revealed the secret Mission gate, the trapper followed the girls all the way back to the Rancho Refugio boundary. Alicia and Nina were more relaxed to be back on the Ortega land, but as soon as the three of them spotted Captain Harris and Clara in the distance the trapper slowed his pace. He held up a finger to his lips, warning the girls to keep silent. He backed away into a brush-covered area and hid himself.

Nina and Alicia thought he was acting strangely, but they were more interested in watching Harris and Clara to see what mischief they were up to. The girls observed them from the shade of a live oak. A flock of rancho sheep grazed nearby.

"Why count stones?" Nina strained to hear his words.

"He's making a picture, a map of Papa's land." Alicia recognized what Captain Harris was doing. She and her papa once followed a surveyor estimating taxes on the land—taxes Papa never paid.

"Twenty-seven, twenty-eight, it's perfect! Leave it all to me, Clara." Harris moved with exaggerated steps and paused near the spot where the stream crossed the pasture. He scribbled something on a parchment Clara held up to him. They headed toward the ridge and continued counting.

"How he make a picture with numbers?" Nina asked. The tensions the girls shared in the village subsided even though the trapper was still nearby.

"Is that man following us?" Alicia could not see the trapper any longer. The girls locked arms to help each other up; they were more interested in observing Harris's movements. He could make his pictures, but he could never trace all 600 acres of Rancho Refugio.

"Clara is helping him." Alicia thought of her sister as a traitor. Did Clara realize she was betraying the entire family by helping Harris to take over their land? "What is he asking her?"

"Where do the cattle graze?" Harris pressed Clara for details about ranching operations. She responded with a shrug of her shoulders. "Where do they do the slaughtering? Who prepares the hides?"

"Just follow your nose, you'll know where they get slaughtered." Alicia and Nina, both nervous, giggled. How could Clara not know that?

Harris and Clara headed toward the coastline. "Shush!" Alicia motioned Nina. Following them was no game.

"Look, the shells," Nina said. "Family sing to ancestors here. Spirits powerful, keep watch on land and village."

"I never noticed those shell mounds before." Alicia learned more about Nina's people.

"Make *tomol boat*, catch sardine, trade here." She searched for words to explain the seashells, burial markers, and warning signs for intruders.

"Your people will not meet here if Harris gets his way."

10
Chapter

At sunset, Harris and Clara prepared to return to the hacienda. Alicia knew they would be hungry and ready for someone to wait on them for dinner. She and Nina moved toward the house, looking from side to side for the trapper.

"Did he leave? Is he around?" Alicia was nervous to have this stranger on the family property.

"Near." Nina appeared certain that he would eventually make himself known.

"I don't like that he followed us. Do you see him?"

"Very near." Nina was the first to reach the cooking ramada and begin the dinner preparations. She scrubbed the garden vegetables with nervous energy.

When Clara and Harris entered the sala they were still chattering and making their plans. Harris examined the papers on the table. He had his own plans for making his fortune in

California. He only shared partial plans with those who could work for his advantage.

"I've figured out how we can use these old parchments, since your papa has no real business papers. A little candle wax and a stamp will make them look official." He grinned like a schoolboy sharing a class project, then spread out all the land measurements and maps from their afternoon's work on the dining table. "I've seen hundreds of ledgers and cargo bills. They are all the same."

Harris gathered all he needed to make his phony ledger look authentic. He thumped across the sala in his muddy boots and pulled two candles from Mama's altar, knocking into Mother Mary's statuette.

Alicia and Nina peered in through the doorway. When the girls saw him approach Mama's altar, they rushed in toward the table.

"What's keeping our dinner, Alicia?" Clara was impatient to show that she was in charge of the house. "It's about time. Get over here and serve our dear Captain Harris," Clara said. Alicia could not stomach her sister's dramatic manners.

"Our dear captain?" Alicia stomped forward with the first small plates of food. She would not let her sister boss her to wait on this man. Nina hesitated at the edge of the sala and kept looking over her shoulder, as if she expected to see the trapper at any time.

"There is only enough dinner for family members," Alicia said.

"How dare you! Apologize this minute," Clara lunged at Alicia and pushed her back out toward the ramada for more food.

"At least you can try to be decent to Captain Harris." Clara hissed in Alicia's face. "He has sacrificed more than you know."

"If you want to eat, leave me alone." Alicia was glad to have an excuse to ignore Clara. "Sacrifice, ha."

"For your information Harris lost his own inheritance to his older brother." Clara dragged out her defense of Harris. "He's suffered and so will you, if you keep being so disrespectful." She nudged Alicia's shoulder, causing dishes to clatter. "Our dear sister, Dolores, ran off to Laredo and left him. I don't blame him if he wants to marry me instead." She returned to the table where Captain Harris waited.

Alicia and Nina looked at each other, eyebrows raised in silence. That last lie about Dolores was a new one. Alicia knew the truth from reading her sister's diary. How convenient for Harris to pretend to be the victim of Dolores's lost love. He had certainly snared Clara, who was new to romance.

When the girls finally entered the sala with more food Harris looked up from his ledger and met Alicia's stubborn expression.

"*Mil gracias.*" Harris offered a sly grin. He realized not all the sisters were gullible. Would he have resistance from the youngest Ortega? "This is perfect, girls. We were hungry." He used flattery and ignored Alicia's rudeness.

Alicia crossed herself and apologized to Mother Mary for Harris's abuses. Could the stories of him losing his family's inheritance be true? What made him such a scoundrel? No matter his so-called suffering, he was still trying to convince Clara to forge documents to take over Papa's land.

"We are worried, Alicia. Your papa is in a lot of trouble and I'm going to help him." He seemed to be reading Alicia's thoughts. "This black-market port owes so many taxes they could throw you off the land." Then Harris blurted out the truth.

"For me, and Clara, this is an opportunity for fame and fortune." They toasted each other to begin their grand scheme. "My brother snatched my inheritance away from me. By God, I am going to outdo him here in this fresh territory and find my land and my fortune." He finished his wine and grabbed the bottle for another pour. "Besides, what can three girls do with the Ortega fortune? You have no business sense and no brother to inherit the property. You need a man like me, a strong young husband, to secure your future."

Nina stood shifting from foot to foot, glancing out toward the garden, still expecting to spot the trapper. Now she reached into her pocket and flicked some of her grandma's protective sand at Harris's muddy boots.

"Oh, bad, bad thing," Nina said. Alicia clutched the seashell Masagawa had given her. "Baba," she thought. Why did Nina's grandma say, "Baba?"

11

Chapter

Harris was absolutely right about some things. The Ortega sisters knew little about the business of ranching. They knew about the vegetable gardens and Mama's precious flower beds. The girls understood kitchen routines, but Nina did the work. Same thing on laundry day. They never scrubbed the linens. The family depended on Chumash skills to make the rancho work.

The table was still spread with the evening meal when an unexpected visitor arrived. Clara and Harris scrambled to cover their mischief-making scheme, the parchments and wax seals strewn around the room.

"Bendiciones todos." A short round man in a brown cassock stood at the door. It was Padre Romo from the Mission, come to give a blessing to the Ortega house, as he had done on many occasions.

"You see, Mother Mary has answered my prayers." Alicia welcomed the arrival of their family friend and spiritual leader, Padre Romo.

"I come forth in the peace of our Lord, with greetings from your family, young ladies." Padre Romo bowed to the sisters. Seeing Captain Harris, he switched from Spanish to English. "How blessed we are that you are here, Captain. You will soon join the Ortega family in holy matrimony, yes? No?" Harris fidgeted and pushed his chair away from Clara.

Alicia wondered how the padre knew just when to arrive. He always seemed to know the business of the family. She retreated to the ramada to collect more food.

"Where's that extra plate?" Alicia grabbed the china plate Mama used for company. Nina appeared from the garden carrying a different plate. When had Nina disappeared to the garden and why?

"No more chicken tonight, just quail," Nina said.

"Chicken, quail, the padre won't notice the difference." Alicia saw Nina sneak some quail onto a plate but did not say anything. Nina often ate alone, away from the family.

Back in the sala, the padre waved a hand to bless the meal, then continued to chatter. His comments were full of news from the parish, the pueblo, and from the Presidio.

"Did that husky trapper bring some special game for dinner?" Fresh quail was a favorite dish of Padre Romo's. He was more interested in the meal than the stranger, but Nina began to blush.

How did the padre already know about the trapper? Is that why Nina was in the garden with a plate? Alicia knew she would have to explain this to Clara.

"What trapper are you referring to?" Clara's voice was full of suspicion. "Alicia, do you know about this?"

"I know nothing about anyone." Alicia lied, picturing the man who made Nina show him the Mission gate.

"I am the only man in the Ortega home these days, Padre." Harris came to Alicia's rescue. His tone was full self-confidence.

Nina's face had an innocent expression as she moved around the table to collect empty plates. Alicia worried about what might happen if the padre found out that Nina showed that trapper the Mission gate.

"He did not appear to be a man of faith. He just rushed past me on the road toward the Mission without a word of greeting." Padre Romo talked while he enjoyed the quail.

"Who are you talking about?" Clara wanted to get to the bottom of this mystery.

"No matter, Brother Lassalle is ready to greet anyone who comes to the Mission tonight. Too many strangers around these days. Have you noticed?"

Alicia agreed with the padre, considering Captain Harris to be one of those unwelcome strangers. She tried to change the subject away from the trapper.

"Is there news from Papa and Mama?" Alicia said. Maybe Romo's news would rid them of Captain Harris. Could the padre be an ally?

"By God's grace, the mail from Laredo arrived at the Mission yesterday. I knew you were hungry for a word from Mama and Papa. And what miraculous news, you won't believe." Clara drew Dolores's shawl around herself, taking on a more grown-up expression.

"Alicia, finish clearing this table. The captain and I will discuss the news with the padre."

"Are they well? When are they coming home?" Alicia could not hold back questions.

"Alicia!" Clara pointed to the pots and baskets. "Go now." There was no polite way to disobey Clara's orders in front of the padre. Alicia and Nina carried away the cook pots, trying to hear the conversation. Moments later, Clara shrieked.

"What! I don't believe it! Do you have the letter? Let me see it."

12

Chapter

"Clara's just putting on an act." Alicia reassured Nina. It was not the first time she had heard her sister being overly dramatic.

Did Padre Romo share news of Dolores's baby? If so, why call it miraculous? It was a serious sin for Dolores and Harris to have a child before they were married. She ran back into the sala.

"What happened, is everything all right?"

"More than all right, dear girl, even if Clara does not recall the story of Abraham and Sarah. Praise God! He still grants children to the faithful in elder years."

"Who is Sarah? What are you saying, Padre Romo?" Alicia often got mixed up about her Bible stories.

"Your Mama and Papa will bring home a new baby in just a few months. Your Mama did not realize she was with child when they left for Laredo. Isn't that a wonderful miracle?" Everyone around the table held their breath.

"Berries!" Nina broke the silence, presenting a bowl of straw-berries. "Eat now?"

"Oh, yes please." The padre helped himself to a new bowl of food. "And there's more news, just business, but it could mean something to your papa." Padre Romo wasted no time, a little berry juice dripping down his chin. "Governor Fages is sending a deputy from Monterey for dock inspections, to make sure all taxes are up to date." The padre leaned forward. "He's sending your uncle, Salvador Tenorio. Maybe as soon as next week!"

Having delivered more earthshaking news than he could have imagined, Padre Romo heaped more fresh berries onto a plate. Clara and Harris did not eat the berries. Nina fanned the flies away from the table, grinning. Alicia glanced up toward Mother Mary and thought, "Baba?"

The after-dinner conversation continued with only one person talking: Padre Romo. He was so used to giving a sermon, a lesson, or an opinion to anyone who would listen, he didn't notice how distracted everyone was.

"Is there coffee?" the padre said.

"*Sí*, coffee." Nina and Alicia shared secret glances across the room. Both knew that Mama and Papa lied about the baby being their own. Clara could not admit the truth about Dolores being pregnant to Padre Romo. Captain Harris seemed more concerned about *Tío* Salvador coming to collect dock taxes. Likely, he did not know the baby being discussed was his child.

"Padre Romo, if Mama's baby is a boy, Papa will have some-one to inherit Rancho Refugio. Is that true?" Alicia glared at Captain Harris.

"Indeed, he will, Alicia. Papa loves you three beautiful girls, but it takes a son to inherit the land. We can only pray that God answers Papa's prayers." Padre Romo had all the answers, all the news and a way of making it sound holy. He was respected by almost everyone.

"The padre knows all about these things. He runs the Mission, you know." Alicia directed her remarks directly to Captain Harris. She was glad to have a grown-up ally on her side for once.

It was true. At the Mission, the padre conducted mass and baptisms and monitored the weaving and wine-making workers. Not only that, he had a knack for spotting cargo from the Orient docked at Refugio. In short, Romo knew everything about everyone in the parish. For the Ortega family he spoke Spanish, the Mass was in Latin, and the Chumash instruction was in some combination of words and gestures. He impressed the Yankees with theological discussions in English. Many settlers arrived as Protestants, then were baptized as Catholics within a month of arrival in *Alta California*. Marriage to a local girl followed weeks later, all sanctioned by Padre Romo.

No one at the table spoke as the padre slurped up the rest of the berries. Then, two men outside interrupted the silence when they came running toward the hacienda calling out in a panic.

"¡Padre, Padre! *¡Fuego!*"

"Now, what?" Clara pushed away from the table. "What fire, where?"

"Bless my soul, *hombres*; we see no fire." Padre Romo rushed out the door and toward the men. Everyone moved out to the patio, sniffing the air and searching the sky. The sun had disappeared, and the hills were dark.

"There is a fire at the back gate of the Mission." Two Chumash men gasped for air after their long run; soot smeared their faces. The padre understood how serious this could be. The Mission's most valuable product, tanned cattle hides, hung to dry near the back gate.

"Harris, you come with me. Was anyone hurt?" Padre Romo rushed to follow the men back onto the Mission trail. Captain Harris followed behind. The coffee remained ignored on the dining table. Nina sneaked out the back door, hoping the trapper had nothing to do with a fire in the exact place she had pointed out to him earlier that afternoon.

13

Chapter

"An unknown trapper seen leaving here, and now a fire at the Mission?" Clara turned on Alicia. "What have you two done that is going to get our family in trouble?"

"I had nothing to do with this," Alicia lied, knowing more than she shared. She looked for Nina, who had disappeared from the patio and the sala.

There was little to do at home after Padre Romo and Captain Harris left to inspect the fire. Alicia washed dishes, with no help from Clara or Nina. A few dishes were missing. Alicia knew she would have time to look for them later. She dragged a blanket near Mama's altar to rest. Clara retreated upstairs, muttering and complaining about ruined plans and the pesky Padre Romo.

Alicia assumed Nina disappeared to warn the trapper. That would get the family in trouble. Was she the same as her brothers, a troublemaker? Why would she sneak off with the man who started the Mission fire? Worse, why take him fresh strawberries on Mama's good china plate?

As the night passed, Alicia lay wide awake, thinking about the second part of Padre Romo's news. It was something about Tío Salvador and taxes. Mama never talked about Tío Salvador. Why pay attention to the ancient family stories? The fun, memorable stories Mama told included exciting events and ended with Papa and the brothers saving shipwrecked sailors from a *Spanish galleon*. Mama liked to tell about their being rewarded with a grant to Rancho Refugio and becoming the heroes of the pueblo.

How did the stories begin? Where did Tío Salvador fit into the family? The Padre said Tío Salvador worked for the governor, assigned to tax collections, an important man.

"Clara, are you still awake? I can't get to sleep." Alicia dared to whisper to her sister in the sleeping loft. "Is Tío Salvador an important man?" She was sure she would get yelled at for waking Clara, but Alicia could not contain her curiosity. "Should I worry about Tío coming to visit Rancho Refugio? I remember nothing about him. Do you?" At first, Clara said nothing.

"I hate to be the one to tell you, but we are in more trouble than you can imagine." Clara lay curled up in a ball. "Do you remember Mama telling us about the feud she had with her cousin, Marie Therese Duran in Monterey?"

"No, I don't remember that. Tell me."

"Mama said that the Duran family, Mama's cousins, always looked down on the Ortegas, suspecting Papa stole gold from that sunken Spanish galleon." Clara covered her face and muffled her words. "Our Papa!" Alicia moved closer, not remembering their last actual conversation without an argument.

"We don't have any gold. I remember Papa and his brothers would make jokes and toasts to Spanish gold at the fiestas. '*A el oro de España*,'" Alicia said.

"Those old toasts may not have been just a joke. Mama's cousin, Maria Theresa, married this man, Salvador Tenorio. Some say Tenorio is an old pirate who bought his position with the governor." Clara sat up and shook a finger in Alicia's face. "Even worse, Tío Salvador is not even Mexican, but Spanish."

"But Padre Romo said the governor of the territory is sending Tío Salvador here to do something about taxes," Alicia said.

"Padre Romo may be the one person who knows the complete story." Clara glared at Alicia. "And he is not likely to tell it."

"I'm confused. What are we supposed to do?" Too many problems piled up on top of one another in Alicia's mind. First, Mama and Papa claimed the new baby was their own. Then there was the news that Tío Salvador planned to come to Refugio to collect back taxes. Now Captain Harris was openly courting Clara. Finally, Alicia was sure Nina ran off to be with the trapper.

"You should have been nicer to Harris, stupid girl. Only he could help us." Clara staggered to her feet and shoved Alicia's shoulder. "What if he does not come back? What will I do?"

"Clara, he doesn't want to help us. Harris just wants the land for himself." Alicia fought back tears. "He wants to lie about all those dock records."

"Oh? Are you telling me that the Ortegas never lie about anything? It's a lie that Mama is having a baby, at her age. That is no miracle." Clara's voice was loud and mean. "And that stupid Indian Nina, she's going to cause us trouble. I'll make sure the padre beats her. Papa should have done that long ago."

"No! They can't. Nina has done nothing wrong. She belongs here with us." Alicia could only fix one problem at a time.

"Just tell me this, little sister. If your friend Nina is so innocent, where is she now?" Clara turned her back and dropped back onto the sleeping mat.

14

Chapter

The next morning Alicia fixed an extra nice breakfast, early, before the coastal fog lifted. Coffee *con leche*, *pan tostado*, scrambled eggs with tiny diced green chiles, and Clara's favorite, *fresas con crema*.

The old dining table was the center of all family activities. It was scrubbed, waxed, and re-scrubbed day after day. The savory aromas of breakfast led Clara to the table, but she was not alone.

"Fresh strawberries and cream," Harris said. "This must be a special day." Noticing that he looked cleaner this morning than last night, Alicia wondered if he used the family's basin and towels. Clara treated him like a regular member of the household and chattered on.

"My sister is practicing all the best dishes to prepare for our Tío Salvador's visit. Isn't that right, little sister?" Clara placed a napkin on her lap. "Isn't it nice that Captain Harris came back to support us?" Alicia noticed that her sister wore work clothes. Why no fancy skirts to parade in front of Captain Harris today?

"The berries are in season. Everyone likes them." It was one of the easiest dishes to make without Nina's help. Alicia watched Clara, imagining what she shared with Captain Harris about their family history discussion last night.

"This Uncle Salvador sounds like a very extraordinary man. I've never heard your papa speak about him," Harris said. He spoke as if he had known Papa forever. "Should we continue with our documents?" Clara must have held back the actual story of Tío Salvador.

"Oh, there's time for all that. Before we do anything else, tell us what happened at the fire. I've always said Alicia is too friendly with Nina and her Indian relations. I told her not to trust them. None of them."

Alicia wrung her hands below the table. Her palms were sweaty. She wanted to ask, was Nina involved with the fire?

"They made arrests. The Presidio soldiers hauled off two fellows," Harris said. "Everyone saw what happened. I can tell you one thing—those boys will be lucky if they get a trial." He spoke like an upstanding citizen full of official news.

"Two of who? Was anyone hurt?" Alicia's breakfast grew cold on her plate.

"I don't know why they didn't arrest that trapper, too. At least they got Nina's thieving brothers," Clara said. "She better not show up here."

"The ruined hides were worth thousands of dollars. I didn't know the Mission made that much money. I'm in the wrong business." Harris stuck out his cleaned plate. "Is there more breakfast?"

"Oh, no you don't. You have work to do." Clara spoke in a tone Mama used with Papa. "That dock needs to look perfect when Tío Salvador gets here. You are the man for the job."

It sounded to Alicia like her sister was trying to keep Harris busy and away from the house. What did she have in mind? He left with an extra piece of toast, and Clara turned to Alicia.

"Leave all this stuff on the table and get your boots on. Don't ask me questions. Just meet me in the garden with a pail and dish towel." Clara had some sort of plan, and it included Alicia.

Alicia's boots were hand-me-down rubbers. After their tenth birthdays, the girls could help Papa work down on the dock. Mama outfitted each of them like a boy with boots, pants, and a slicker jacket. A knit cap covered their curls. It was a disgrace to set young girls to the type of work Papa did at the dock, but the Ortegas had no son to learn Papa's trade. After a few years of dirty chores, Alicia's sisters refused the scummy dock jobs and claimed young ladies were only fit for petticoats and pinafores.

For Alicia, the rubber boots meant freedom and adventure. When her feet jammed against the toes, Papa split open the ends of the boots to fit her. She still wore the boots with pride and pulled them on, not knowing where they would lead her today.

"Where are you, Clara?" Alicia surveyed the garden.

"Shush! Over here." Clara waved from beyond the potato vines, standing beside the tool shack. She held her bucket and a rag.

"Why are we being quiet? There's no one here but us." Alicia hoped to glimpse Nina somewhere on the grounds. She scanned all their favorite hiding places.

"Follow me. I don't want Harris to see us." Clara made her way down toward the shoreline. Alicia and Nina knew this portion of the beach well. The stretch of sand lay far from the dock. Alicia used the pathway frequently with Nina. It led to the hidden cave, a hideaway they used for storing treasures and secrets. That cave held many happy memories. Was that where Nina hid?

Alicia always assumed her sisters did not know about the spot. They never ventured away from the hacienda. Alicia slowed down on purpose and pretended to be interested in the plants.

"Look, more strawberries growing along the pathway. Did you know?" Alicia bent to pick the fruit and put it in her pail.

"Leave them be. That's not why we are here. This is a family secret," Clara said.

15

Chapter

What family secret would Clara share today? Alicia believed Nina hid in the cave, maybe with the trapper. But she didn't want to admit her suspicions to Clara.

"Does this path lead to the beach?" Alicia played ignorant. "Let me go first. It may get slippery." She tried to move around Clara, but her sister took a firm grip on her wrist.

"So, you have been down this pathway before?" Clara grew suspicious. A moment passed, then they both knew the truth.

"Alicia?" Nina stood on the beach and the trapper stood close to her. They were very near the mouth of the special cave.

"What are they doing here?" Clara said.

"Nina! We've been so worried about you." She was right. This is where Nina hid. Shame on her. She looked perfectly content, but so young, at the trapper's side.

"I—" Nina took the slightest step forward and spoke.

"Why run off with this man?" Alicia was stern, trying to shield Nina from Clara's wrath. After two days and nights, Nina still wore her flour sack apron.

"Shame on you for deceiving us and running away. Do you recognize what he has done?" Clara was angry and suspicious. She turned on Alicia. "You knew she was here. You always protect her."

"We—" Nina held up her hands in surrender.

"Speak up!" Alicia clutched the old bucket and towel and wondered why Clara had asked for these things.

"Ladies, if you will allow me." It was only the second time Alicia heard the trapper speak. He seemed to be done with his hiding, and unafraid. He wore the leather leggings and rabbit-fur cap Alicia had seen him wearing in the village. His voice was serious and precise, as if he were addressing a public meeting.

"I want to know what you are doing on our land. Who informed you about this cave?" It was hard to tell what made Clara so distraught. Was it the fact that Nina ran away? Or was she upset to have a bold stranger on their land? Clara stood in front of the cave and pushed the others back.

When Nina's voice came to her, her expression changed from timid to daring. She showed no shame or surprise at being found.

"This trapper, he knows all herbs, good like Grandma Masagawa." Nina looked from the trapper to Clara.

"I am a sergeant and surveyor, Miss. You have this wrong." When the trapper spoke, Alicia realized he was not the ignorant ruffian she'd assumed.

"Don't say another word. You are trespassing on our family property." Clara strode toward him, swishing her arms as if she was shooing chickens. "Get away from here."

"We just needed a protected place," the trapper said.

"Only because you set fire to the Mission." Clara did not back down. This stranger tried to talk his way out of his crime.

"I am not responsible for that fire. I was there, counting hides, but I didn't start the fire." The trapper was now face-to-face with Clara. Alicia saw her sister fighting for control. The tall stranger could not intimidate her.

"He no set fire," Nina said. "My brothers, drunk and *loco*."

"Just sit down right where you are. Tell me your story." Clara exhaled her exasperation. She eyed Nina and the trapper then shifted her glance to the cave.

"Trapper make pictures with numbers. Like Captain Harris." Nina bragged about the trapper. When she spoke up in his defense, Alicia felt a twinge of jealousy to notice the admiration on her friend's face.

"Don't talk about Captain Harris. It's maps he makes, you stupid girl." Clara did not realize Nina observed them from afar. Alicia knew she referred to Harris plotting their land.

"Survey maps. That is my job." The trapper faced Clara. Nina sat behind him. "For instance, what are you collecting with those buckets, crabs?" His natural curiosity unsettled Clara and Alicia. "I'm making a survey: land, plants, animals. Part of the Western exploration. It's my job."

"Be honest with me, mister, did you take anything from this cave?" There was something enraging Clara, the closer she came to that cave.

16

Chapter

When would life ever return to normal times? Alicia realized that each day Mama and Papa were away brought new problems, new people, and new worries to Rancho Refugio. The trapper continued to make his case.

"I'm not stealing anything." He continued in a calm tone and asked more questions about the ranch, the land, and shoreline, as if he was conducting his own inspection. Alicia wondered who he actually worked for. He was not Spanish or Mexican. Was he some kind of spy?

Clara had met her match. She kept protesting, trying to intimidate the trapper. He appeared amused that she was so agitated.

"Run down to the dock, Alicia. Fetch Captain Harris. He'll march this fellow to the Presidio and get the truth." Alicia couldn't ignore her sister's command. She realized there was something bigger that worried Clara, so she headed toward the dock to get Harris.

Even from afar she could observe the dock's planks, the twisted ropes, hooks, and floats all lined up in order. Not like Papa kept them. A tattered Mexican flag hung from a pole Harris scrounged from the trash and timbers strewn on the beach. Harris was doing his best to make the harbor look presentable, probably for Tío Salvador's inspection.

"Captain Harris, Clara wants to speak with you." Alicia did not thank him for his work or show any sign of appreciation. "There's a man. A mapmaker." At this moment Alicia distrusted both Harris and the trapper.

"I could certainly use his help. Where's the man from?" Harris squinted down the beach, his hand shading his eyes. He was in no hurry. "Can you help me with this?"

"No, I'm not your dockhand. I told you, Clara wants to see you right now."

"I can see you are just as spoiled as your sisters." Harris stood, legs astride, facing Alicia. "None of you understand how the rancho works or how to manage the land. You girls need a brother, a man to take care of business."

"Will you explain it all to me, just like you explained it to my sisters?" Harris might fool Dolores and Clara, but Alicia would never lift a finger to help him steal Rancho Refugio away from the family. "I know Papa saved the sailors, and the government gave him this land." Alicia folded her arms across her chest to emphasize her confidence. "They expect him to work the land and pay taxes each year."

"And he's barely done one of those things. He must produce those back taxes in full or lose the land." Harris took a step toward her.

"Don't be so certain of yourself. Papa has his ways." Alicia hoped she was right.

"And I have mine. I know that the blood relative clearing the debt will own the grant. That will be Clara, and me, as her husband." Harris jumped off the dock onto the sand, looking extremely proud of himself.

"Not if I can stop you. Not if someone pays the debt first." Alicia needed to keep her own plan secret. "Your lies and false records will not save you, Captain Harris."

"Calm down, Alicia, I've already lost one family, fighting over land." He turned to look at her and tried another approach. "Let's work together." Tío Salvador's arrival could be any day. Harris and Clara were ready to present their elaborate ledger books, every page a lie.

"Enough talk. Clara is waiting for you now." As soon as Harris moved out of sight, Alicia inspected all he accomplished. He had actually made the dock presentable with the faded flag whipping in the ocean breeze. If only she could pay the taxes, they could host official ships. Maybe the family would gain respect, and the dock would not be a black market for pirates and thieves.

Those minutes walking along the dock alone gave Alicia a new idea. Maybe Tío Salvador's visit could help them catch up with their taxes and save Rancho Refugio for the Ortega family.

Alicia paced out to the edge of the dock and back toward the beach. Beneath the dock boards a unique sound, a crunch, echoed with each step. She had never noticed it before. Looking under the pilings, she could see that her family had built the dock on a pile of shells. Was this one of the shell mounds Nina told her about? Nina's ancestors' burial place? A holy place? A chilling spirit fell over Alicia.

17

Chapter

Alicia needed time alone. Everyone else—Clara, Harris, Nina, and the trapper—returned to the hacienda for the evening meal. After dinner, Harris would take the trapper to the Presidio. Alicia was relieved to have Nina back home to cook.

The dock at sunset was a magical place, and Alicia sat alone there with her thoughts and memories. The crunch of the shell mound below the planks and the view of the crashing waves consumed her imagination. Finally, she had time, alone, to work out her private thoughts about the family secrets.

Who kept all the secrets in the pueblo, she wondered? Accusations of Papa and his brothers stealing Spanish gold haunted her thoughts. It could not be true. What happened when the Spanish galleon smashed into these rocks at Refugio over thirty years ago?

She remembered the stories her mother shared when she was a little girl. Mama told her daughters the romantic version of the tale where the Ortega brothers scrambled down from their lookout post and hauled many Spanish sailors to safety before their splintered ship sank. The entire pueblo celebrated their bravery and mourned the loss of those who went down with the ship. Mama's story was always the same.

"Was the ship ever found under the ocean?" Little Alicia used to ask.

"Found? Child, you know how deep the bay is, how strong the tides are." Mama never mentioned a word about gold. She told about the honors and the land grant. "And that land is where we sit today because of your Papa's bravery."

"But those are big ships. We see them at the military port. How could it disappear?" Alicia or Clara would always beg for more of the story. But even as a girl, Dolores was never curious.

"You can always ask old Ernesto," Mama once said.

"Yuck, old Ernesto? The *borracho*? The drunk? You tell us to never look up when we see him in town," the younger girls would say.

"That's true, but he was one of the rescued sailors. He worships your papa. The others have all moved away now or died."

"Or they are drunks," Clara liked to say. Alicia shared Clara's suspicions when she grew more savvy.

Now that she was older, no longer an innocent child, Alicia could not bring herself to believe the scandalous rumors of Papa's gold that Clara overheard from Tío Salvador's rich, spoiled wife, Maria Theresa. As the stars began to appear over the dock Alicia had a new idea about how she would solve these mysteries.

There was another adult to ask. The only one who might remember. A person sworn to honesty. It was Padre Romo. Alicia would make a plan to see him and have a grown-up talk. She had to do it before Tío Salvador arrived to inspect Papa's port and discover the missing taxes.

By the time Alicia reached the hacienda, the trapper sat chatting with the others at the family table. Harris had not hauled him off to the Presidio as Clara had instructed. Instead, Harris talked to him as if they were old friends. The trapper told stories about his travels all around the territory. Alicia talked to Clara and explained her plan to see Padre Romo.

"I don't see why you have to go to the Mission. Not before we have everything ready for Tío Salvador's arrival," Clara complained.

"I'll go to confession," Alicia said.

"What does a fourteen-year-old have to confess?" Clara said. "Tell him how lazy and unladylike you are."

"Well, I'm going. Just because you never confess don't try to stop me."

"Me? Confess? Ha!"

18

Chapter

Alicia took time to plan the perfect conversation with Padre Romo. The next day she walked along the Mission path thinking of all her questions and how to ask them. The padre expected her confession, not an inquisition about a sunken Spanish galleon.

"Bless me Padre, for I have sinned." She practiced using the words for confession, then lingered in the back of the church where small rooms joined by a curtained window separated the padre and repentant sinners. When she saw *señora* Marino exit the tiny room, crossing herself, Alicia darted in. The bench was still warm from señora Merino's steamy confession.

"Go on, my child," Padre Romo said.

"I have been disobedient to my parents and dishonest to my sister."

"The scriptures tell us to honor our father and mother." Padre Romo reminded her of things she already knew. "You must be honest with your sister. Is this Clara?"

"Sí, Padre, Clara."

"Do unto others," Padre Romo said. "You would not want Clara to tell you lies, would you?"

"But, Padre, I'm confused by things she told me." Alicia eased into her actual questions.

"What things are these, my child?"

"Clara said some people think Papa is a thief. That he stole."

"Stop right there. You dishonor your parents by saying such things." Padre Romo's voice changed from its normal mildness to a tone so rough there was no doubt the others waiting in the church heard him. "Say three Hail Mary's and four Our Fathers!"

"But Padre. I need to talk to you," Alicia said.

"Not here. Others are waiting to confess. After the noon meal, meet me in the garden and we can talk. Now go say your prayers, young lady." Alicia squeezed back out of the tiny closet of a room. Those waiting lifted their eyebrows with curiosity when she passed. She slunk toward the altar and knelt on a folded shawl on the dirt floor to begin her prayers.

The Mission gardens were the most peaceful place. After saying her prayers, Alicia waited and noticed the gardeners who tended the plants. She knew how much work it took to keep the flowers blooming and the pathways clear. Their home garden was much bigger than this space, but the air here held a calm spirit that lulled Alicia into believing everything the clerics taught.

The Chumash workers assigned to the yard bent over the flower patches. Big floppy hats shaded their faces. These were Nina's people. They were not as cheery as the people Alicia saw in the village. They wore long baggy pants and stained shirts. Some used a bright *cinturón*, a belt, to hold up their pants.

"Ah, here you are." The padre approached on a garden path.

"I have waited and said my required prayers, Padre."

"Did you say them or did you also feel them, Alicia?" Padre Romo examined the girl's face. "You still seem troubled to me."

"No, no. I am okay, but I do have questions." Alicia had a line prepared to say. "You have a wonderful memory for prayers and scripture. I know you have a splendid memory of the pueblo, too."

"It is the job of a padre, Alicia, to hear confessions, to absolve and then forget." Padre Romo sat next to her. "Your mama and papa, your uncles too, have as many memories here as I do." His words made Alicia's heart beat fast. Would he be straightforward with her?

"Tell me about when you first met them. When you were all young."

"Do you think us all so old today?" Padre Romo smiled and wagged his finger at Alicia.

"I just want to imagine all of you at my age," Alicia said.

"I cannot go that far back." Padre Romo scanned the Mission roof line that needed repairs. Then his gaze went higher, toward the clouds. "I was a young novitiate, and the Ortega brothers were military scouts posted up on the Refugio Ridge, almost in the same spot where you live today. Your mama was young and beautiful."

Alicia could see the padre remembering the days before he had all his Mission responsibilities, before she and Clara were born, even before Dolores's christening.

"Was there a shipwreck?" Alicia blurted out her question.

"That was a very sad day. A dark memory that I dislike recalling."

"But it happened here, just as they say?" Alicia said.

"It happened. But each man tells the story in his own way." Romo's eyes left sky gazing and looked on the pebbled pathway. "Those were sad times. Your papa was a hero, Alicia, but many died."

"And they never found the wreck? Is that true?"

"That was the devil's own storm, young lady. Nothing survived. Only those your papa saved by the grace of God." Romo glanced over the garden area. "I heard your confession this morning. Perhaps God sent you to hear my confession." Alicia shifted on the bench. She sat up straight, searching the padre's face.

"I could never hear your confession, Padre." She shook her head, not wanting to appear too curious.

19

Chapter

Alicia, wide-eyed, sat wondering if she would really hear the padre's confession. Romo soothed her with his words in Spanish.

"*Cálmate, mijita.* All you need to do is listen."

"Well, I can listen." She hoped he would not change his mind but would go on with a story that she could tell Clara.

"And another thing, you can never share what I tell you, just as I never share the confessions of others," Romo explained. "You want to know our history, and that shipwreck has a lot to do with our story." At last, it sounded as if he would answer her questions, even if she could not share his exact words with Clara.

"Were you there? Did you see it?"

"The Mission was small and drafty in those times. They assigned me to shore up the gaps in the walls during the terrible storm. It was only when the survivors arrived in town that I learned of the tragedy. It was awful." Romo wrung his hands as he spoke. "They brought the sailors in on buckboards." Alicia tried to imagine Papa's buckboard filled with wounded men. "There were twelve survivors. Poor souls. *Fíjate*, just twelve out of one hundred."

Romo looked from side to side as if he was reliving the grim procession. Alicia felt sick in her stomach to hear him recount the night. It was not an exciting story, just grim.

"In those days, some Mission brothers had medical skills. They tended to the men, but there was not much they could do to mend their crushed bodies." Romo pointed to a corner of the yard. "We lay them there, under a leaky ramada."

"Why so few saved?" Alicia pictured Papa struggling to save the sailors in the water.

"The ship crashed. They say that all the cargo broke loose." Romo retold the tale as it was shared with him. "Your papa rushed in and out of the icy water many times. Your uncles, too. Those men thrown into the ocean got pulled under by the current and drawn out to sea." Alicia knew those waters and could not imagine such horror. "The heavy cargo crates sunk in the shallows." This grabbed her attention, imagining the tragedy. The bodies washed out to sea, and the trunks lodged in the sandy shallows.

"And what was in those trunks, Padre? Is it true that the galleon held Spanish gold?" Alicia felt the guilt of her curiosity.

"That was one story." Romo looked at Alicia. "But it is only the survivors who know for sure."

"What did they say?" She wanted to know if Papa had touched those trunks. Perhaps he saved the cargo before the men and that was why only twelve survived.

"Only one man is alive to speak of it. You see, after a week, half of the survivors passed on to heaven." The padre continued to speak until the sun moved from the garden and the air grew cooler. Alicia knew she would be late returning home, but she wanted to hear every detail.

"They transferred three men to Monterey. Two deserted once they regained their strength. The last survivor, Ernesto, is a confused drunkard."

"Has he always been like that? Was he ever sober?" Alicia remembered seeing Ernesto staggering down the street. Mama scolded her for making fun of him.

"*Pobrecito*, that man is always loyal to your papa, sober or tipsy." Romo shifted to face Alicia. "Here is my confession: someone sent contributions to the Mission for the survivors. Then, they sent even more *regalitos* whenever the pueblo was in need. Some secret donor still sends us money to take care of poor Ernesto."

"I don't understand. Why is that your confession, Padre?"

"They always send wrapped pieces of gold. Spanish gold," Padre Romo said.

The truth of gold from the shipwreck was confirmed, but the mystery of who hid it remained.

20

Chapter

"Someone here in our pueblo has the gold, and you don't know who?" Alicia needed to discover who had the gold and beg them to pay Papa's back taxes before he lost the land grant. After all, her papa was a hero.

"I should not have burdened you with my little secrets. You have your own mysteries to solve. Are you all ready for your Tío Salvador's visit?"

"Should I be worried about that? I know he is coming to collect taxes. What else can you tell me about him?" Alicia said.

"Follow me to my desk; I'll show you something."

Alicia knew the Mission's chapel and gardens, but Padre Romo led her into another corner of the building. It was dim and smelled musty. She expected the padre to have a much nicer space. They wedged into the small office and Padre Romo unrolled a cracked parchment on his desktop: a map.

"I love to look at maps. What does this show?" The map was faded, blotched with water spots and ink spills. "I see us here, Alta California. It's so tiny." She touched the spot, but Padre Romo brushed her hand away.

"Look, this is where Salvador Tenorio comes from." Padre Romo held down the right edge of the map and pointed to a speck marked, "*Cadíz*." His finger traced above the parchment map all the way to Refugio. "Your uncle was not much older than you when he arrived here with our Mission founder, a Franciscan named Padre Serra."

"Was my tío a religious man, like you?"

"Your uncle's pathway took many turns, but now he serves the governor of our territory, and he is due to arrive here any day." Alicia wondered what turns in his passage the padre referred to, but she did not seek an explanation. "Remember, I told you some men from the wreckage were taken to Monterey? Salvador was in Monterey when those survivors arrived."

The padre's stories were still in her mind when Alicia approached the hacienda at twilight. She looked out to the ocean, imagining the sunken ship, the drowned sailors, and chests of gold.

"I have so much to tell you." Alicia burst into the sala but was immediately hushed by Clara.

"It's about time. Where have you been? You have work to do. Nina has left us again. Following that trapper, God knows where."

"We've been waiting for you to finish preparations for our guest. Your sister is busy helping me." Harris was still there at the house. He lifted up his false ledger book. "We have finished our official records for your uncle to review."

"I am sure our tío is delayed in Monterey. Is that your announcement or do you have anything else worth hearing?"

Alicia did not want to share her stories in front of Harris, so she said her goodnights and curled up with a blanket next to the fire.

After the candles burned out, a wagon rattled along the pathway near the house. An off-key singer belted out a sorrowful song,

"*La vida no vale nada.*" Only Clara and Alicia heard the racket. Nina and the trapper now slept at the village near Grandma Masagawa. Harris slept near the loft.

"*Entrando cuando llorando,*" a second singer chimed in. Harris rushed into the room, a handgun in his grip. He dashed to the front door.

"Careful, sounds like drunkards." Harris blocked Alicia as she tried to peek outside. Had Nina's brothers, Pedro and Flaco, escaped from the jail? Were they coming here looking for their sister?

"I think it's only old Ernesto, drunk again. Singing one of his salon songs." Alicia recognized him. "Wait. He's got someone with him in the wagon."

"That's disgusting." Clara hated to have her beauty sleep interrupted. "Get rid of him, Harris." Who was that stranger? Harris readied himself to shoot his pistol at the intruders.

"Wait!" Alicia said. "They don't seem to be dangerous, just drunk."

"Why would a couple of drunks wander by? What are they doing around here?" Clara hobbled downstairs in her yellow sleeping gown, not even embarrassed that Harris saw her in her nightclothes.

21

Chapter

"Fa–mil–i–a!" a cry rang out. "Your favorite uncle has arrived!"

"Oh my Lord, this can't be!" Clara flew to her loft, pulled on a coat, then returned and pushed Alicia and Harris aside. "Tío Salvador?"

In person, Salvador seemed sober, the perfect representative of the governor. His clothes were wrinkled but very dignified. Harris rushed to straighten his own tangled hair and tuck his nightshirt into his baggy pants. Alicia grabbed her blanket and draped it over her shoulders like a *rebozo*. Clara summoned her most welcoming smile.

"At last, Tío. *Bienvenido!* It is late, but good to see you here." Clara frowned at Ernesto who wobbled in the driver's seat of the wagon. He was still humming his tune.

"*A sus órdenes.* Is that the eldest Ortega daughter, Dolores speaking?" Salvador stood in the doorway. "*Disculpe*, my apologies, to disturb your peace." He had only met the girls as infants and did not know Harris. "I ran into an old friend in the pueblo. You know Ernesto, yes? We shared stories of the old days." He let his fashionable jacket fall to the ground and waved toward Ernesto, who reached for a valise and carried it into the sala.

Everyone stepped backward to give him plenty of room. Ernesto's black hooded cape made him look like a giant bat. He breathed hard, stank of liquor, and kept his head down, not looking anyone in the eye.

"*Hola,* Ernesto." Only Alicia offered her hand to greet him by name. She could not remember any other time he dared to visit the Ortega home.

"Tío, I am Clara. This is my little sister Alicia and our dear family friend Captain Harris." She did her best to take charge of the unexpected arrival and ignored Ernesto's awkward presence. "I'm sure you will welcome a good rest after your long journey. We have everything prepared for you."

Salvador put his hand on the drunkard's shoulder. "We met years ago when your papa rescued his shipmates and brought some injured men to Monterey. So many stories, eh?"

"Yes, but it is so late." Clara wanted the drunk removed.

"Not too late to ask after your mama and papa." Tío Salvador slowed down Clara's hastiness. "Oh yes, they are off to Laredo with your older sister, true?"

"They are all fine, thank you. Captain Harris, if you please."

"Let me assist you to your wagon, Ernesto." Harris interpreted Clara's instructions, removing the drunk from the house.

"*Adiós,*" everyone muttered. "*Buenas noches.*" Salvador followed the other two men to the wagon. The sisters were alone for a moment.

"What did you expect me to do?" Clara rubbed the backs of her hands, ridding herself of Ernesto's contamination.

22

Chapter

"They're friends, our tío and Ernesto, didn't you know?" Alicia showed off her newfound knowledge. She imagined the stories Ernesto and Tío Salvador shared about the old days.

"Tío Salvador may be the only one who can answer your questions about the past." Clara washed off everything she imagined old Ernesto had touched. "Harris and I have our plans all worked out. We'll show him our ledger tomorrow. Make sure you do nothing to ruin it."

No one in the house slept that night except Tío Salvador. His snores sounded like a thunderstorm. Clara and Harris worried about the next day's conversation with him. Alicia lay awake imagining the worst about what he might know of the shipwreck and the gold. She giggled to herself, recalling his unexpected arrival and the look of shock on Clara's face.

The rooster crowed long before anyone wanted to hear him. Alicia rolled over, still caught up in a dream. In it she and

Nina were in the special cave and Nina served her tea to soothe her spirit.

"Oh! My stomach!" Now awake, Alicia curled into a ball, hugging her knees to her chest. Her sheets were sticky and wet. She wiped her hand on her thigh and saw the blood collecting between her legs.

"Nina, come help me." She called out, forgetting that Nina was not in the house. How could she move, much less clean herself up and begin the breakfast preparations? I made blood—like a woman, she said to herself.

"Tea? Special tea for you." Nina appeared at her bedside, just like in her dream.

"Are you truly here?"

"Take. Hot. You make blood," Nina said. "Me too. Tea hot." She put down a cup next to Alicia and drew clean rags out of her pocket. She knew just what to do.

"But Tío. He is here," Alicia stammered.

"In garden with trapper now. We come early; I fix breakfast." She took Alicia's sheets for cleaning and brought her fresh clothing.

"Bless you. Thank you." Alicia sipped her soothing tea. "How did you know? I dreamed of us in our cave." In the care of her friend, Alicia's pains lessened.

"You and me." Nina nodded toward the clean rags and showed Alicia how to fold them.

"Why so much pain?" Alicia said.

"Make space for baby," Nina said. Could Alicia trust her information? It seemed like she was leaving something unsaid. "Tell me dream."

"Do you remember the time we were collecting shells in the cave and you discovered that coin?" She had not recalled this earlier. "Remember how mad Papa got when we showed it to him?"

"Very mad," Nina said. She nodded as if she could see the memory.

"After that we let no one know we played there." Alicia remembered how suspicious Clara got when Nina and the trapper stayed at the cave. "Do you think . . . ?" She could not imagine that the Spanish gold was in their special cave.

"I come again tomorrow. We sleep at night with Masagawa in village." Then Nina was gone, and Alicia heard Clara and Tío Salvador in the sala. She forced herself to join them, still in pain with her cramps.

Nina returned each morning to help Alicia that first week of Tío's visit, always wearing the same skirt and apron. Alicia wondered how she did the work, stayed in the village, and appeared again each morning. Nina made Alicia promise, in exchange for her help, that she would attend her brother's trial.

It was all the pueblo talked about. "Indians on trial for burning Mission!" Nina needed Alicia's support and protection. The sensational news traveled along the coast and into the villages. Alicia hoped Tío Salvador would finish his business before the trial began. But her uncle did not seem in any hurry to conduct his business.

He rose early, strolling the grounds and the dock each day in elegant boots, gray striped pants, and a dark vest over his white silk shirts. The first morning, he and the trapper talked at length. The next day Captain Harris walked the grounds with him, no doubt trying to ingratiate himself.

Clara exhausted herself trying to be gracious. Alicia cooked and cleaned, grateful for Nina's help. After the noon dinner, Tío Salvador lay down for a lengthy *siesta* and began his thunderstorm of snores all over again. Each evening he lit silver candlesticks before dinner.

23

Chapter

"What is he doing?" Clara was beside herself with anxiety. "Did you show him the ledger?" She badgered Harris, who remained sullen and quiet. What was Tío Salvador thinking about the family land grant?

On Sunday, he joined the girls for morning prayers at Mama's altar. After prayers, he invited Alicia to stroll with him. Clara glared, no doubt thinking she had the right, as the older sister, to go with Tío.

As Alicia and Salvador walked in the rancho hills he asked, "Do you like your life here, Alicia? Would you like to visit other places?" Was it a trick? Did he plan to make the whole Ortega family move from their homeland?

"This is our home, and I love it," Alicia said. "I also love to learn stories about the early days with Mama and Papa and you and *Tía* Maria Theresa in Monterey."

"You do? Why do you want to hear stories about old folks?" Tío Salvador teased her. "What is it you wish to know?" He was a patient man and waited for her reply.

They walked to the ridge overlooking the hillside. From there they looked out at the Pacific and the tattered flag Harris placed on Papa's dock. Alicia wanted to ask about Papa and his brothers saving Spanish sailors. But she bit her lip and remained silent, pretending to watch the seagulls.

"I can tell you this: we were all poor. Well, all but Maria Theresa and her papa, *señor* Duran in Monterey." So, that much of Clara's story was true. It was his wife who had money.

"We worked to get by. Your papa and his *hermanos* served as lookouts for the Spanish ships. Your mama served the officers' wives at the Presidio. They met and fell in love."

"Mama has told us that much. And you, Tío?" Alicia said.

"I was taken in by a kind Franciscan brother who lived with the Natives. By the grace of God, he saved my life," Salvador said. Alicia noticed he said nothing about being a Spaniard nor a pirate. "By the time your parents met, I was in Monterey meeting my wife."

"You were not here for the . . . ?" She hesitated to say shipwreck. "You did not meet old Ernesto in our pueblo?"

"A-li-ci-a! *¡Cena!*" Clara's voice rang out, announcing the noon meal. "*Adelante.* Come now." She interrupted at the worst time, rushing toward them wearing a ruffled apron, one that Mama always saved for holidays. She carried a kitchen towel— the first Alicia could ever remember seeing her hold.

"You and I must walk together on another day, Clara. Perhaps tomorrow," Tío Salvador said. "I'll tell you about the capital in Monterey. You would find much to do there."

"It would be my pleasure, of course," Clara said. "To walk with you tomorrow, I mean."

"Then we will do so. Alicia and I will follow you back to the house while we finish today's conversation." Salvador had a direct way of letting Clara know she had interrupted them. Alicia saw the anger in Clara's eyes. They followed her at a slow pace.

"I found something on my walk yesterday. Perhaps you would like it, Alicia." Tío Salvador withdrew something from his vest pocket and slipped it into her hand. It was a small gold coin.

Harris chose this mealtime to display the fake ledger book to Tío Salvador. He was more dressed up than Alicia had ever seen him. He wore a captain's suit and cap, clean boots, and a clean shave. No doubt Clara pressured him into this.

"It's very simple, but perhaps you will find the records helpful in your work here, sir," Harris said. How clever, Alicia thought.

"I thank you, Captain Harris. You are a man of the sea. I'm sure you know the importance of such logs." Tío Salvador turned the pages. Some pages stuck together, still damp from their recent creation. "Very interesting, indeed." Tío Salvador took his time looking at the book.

"*Comida*?" Clara cooed. "A special meal for a special guest." She piled her uncle's plate with food and hoped he would retire for his siesta soon.

"You have genuine talents, Clara." Tío Salvador sounded sincere. "Your mama and papa must be proud of you. All of you." He finished his meal without another word about Harris's ledger and then closed himself off for a long afternoon nap. He left the book, with its sticky pages, on the dining table.

"That was the best you could do?" Clara thumped her fist on the ledger when Tío Salvador was out of earshot. "Pages sticking together?" Clara snatched Harris's half-finished meal from him. "This meal is over for you."

"Excuse me. I'll clean up later." Alicia needed to get to away and investigate the cave. Where had Tío Salvador found that gold coin?

Tío slept all afternoon in his room at the back of the hacienda with the door closed. Harris sat alone on the dock, tending ropes and nets. He hid from Clara and her scorn. The ledger had not impressed Tío Salvador and Harris needed to devise an alternative plan.

Alicia slipped out of her company clothing and pulled on a pair of her garden pants. She suspected her dream about collecting shells with Nina in their secret cave meant something special. She tucked her hair into a knit cap like a sneakthief. All she could think of was that gold coin her tío found and her dream. When the house was quiet, Alicia headed out to the cave.

"What took you so long?" Much to Alicia's surprise, Clara was already waiting at the mouth of the cave. She wore a heavy work apron over her dress. Her stockings were smudged with dirt. The buckets and rags, left last week, sat on the rocks. "You are so stupid; I can't believe you are my sister."

"What do you mean?" Alicia, wide-eyed, mustered a casual tone. "When did you get here?"

"Grab your bucket and follow me. You look like you are dressed for a costume party." Clara entered the cool damp cave. "By the way, *feliz cumpleaños*; happy birthday."

"It's not my—" Alicia stopped walking. In all the commotion, she had forgotten. "Not just my birthday, my *quinceanera*!" The fifteenth birthday was special for all the girls. It was the year they were celebrated, not as children, but as young ladies.

"Mama knew she might miss your special day," Clara said.

"She knew?" Alicia felt so let down. The other sisters had big parties for their fifteenth birthdays. "Did she leave me something?"

Chapter

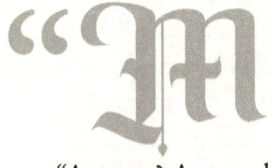ama left you the same thing she gave me and Dolores for our birthdays." Clara walked ahead, further back into the cave than Alicia and Nina had ever dared.

"A party? A new dress? Some present?"

"Does this look like a party to you, little sister?" Clara tugged at the wall of the cave. A heavy tarp, like the ones Papa used on the dock, pulled away from the rocks. A dark, splintered box lay in the shadows. Alicia held her breath.

"Is that my present? Is it what I think?" She was excited but did not want to discover her papa might be a thief. "What is it?"

"It is the family secret that Dolores and I both learned when we turned fifteen. Mama wanted you to know, too." Clara said. "It is the gold from the shipwreck."

"Then the rumors are true? Papa is a thief? Will he go to prison if anyone finds out?" Alicia wished she did not know the truth.

"He saved the sailors, and he recovered the gold, too. I heard the story direct from Papa. He is no thief. The gold was meant for the pueblo and the Mission. He did not turn it over to those who already had so much more than the poor people."

"But he lied." Alicia did not want to think of her papa in this way.

"He used it to care for the survivors. Then he was made a hero and given the land. How could he tell anyone he saved it?" Clara told the story the way her parents had told it to her. "Mama and Papa gave away little portions to those in need, secretly. Later, Padre Romo helped them meet the needs of the poor and the church."

"Does Padre Romo know where it came from?" Romo had as much as told Alicia the truth in his confession.

"At fifteen we were sworn to secrecy, and now so are you." Clara said. "Here, give me that bucket. We have work to do." Clara reached into the box and pulled out three handfuls of old coins. She let them fall to the bottom of her bucket. On top, she arranged a towel to hide the coins. "Now it's your turn."

"This is how you do it?" Alicia approached the box as if there was a wild animal inside. "Actual gold in these old buckets? What if someone sees?" She followed her sister's example.

"Here, fill the bucket with these." Clara dragged a burlap bag full of empty mussel shells toward her bucket.

"These are like the shells we crush for the garden."

"Every time we visit here, we have shells for the backyard." Clara lifted her bucket and pushed it toward her sister. "Hurry."

"What are we going to do with . . . it?" Alicia whispered. She could not say the word "gold" out loud. "With the shells?"

"I think Padre Romo needs them for his garden, don't you?"

The mystery of where the Spanish gold was hidden was solved. Now Alicia had to face a new problem: how they were going to use this gold to pay Papa's back taxes.

The old buckets sat in the garden for several days until the girls could get away. For the moment, everyone was distracted by the coming trial of Nina's brothers. Alicia was nervous that someone would empty the buckets out for water or some other chore, but these days only she and Clara did chores around the hacienda. Harris was fretting about his ledger and trying to be extra friendly. His fine captain's uniform was getting more wrinkled each day. Tío Salvador continued to take his regular walks and naps.

Meanwhile the trial of Nina's brothers was getting under-way. The trapper, feeling like he was to blame for getting the brothers involved in his work, was publicly outspoken.

"Damned fools. This backward town has got it all wrong." The trapper opposed the trial of Pedro and Flaco for starting the fire. In the early morning hours, a crowd was gathering in anticipation of the event. The trapper complained while Nina helped Masagawa find a place to rest in the pueblo. They arrived at eight in the morning and waited until the afternoon. Everyone knew about the case. The brothers were being tried for burning two hundred and fifty cowhides to a crisp.

"The hides are the primary source of funds for us." Padre Romo had reluctantly pressed charges, and now the trial was beginning.

"Why didn't they just arrest me? Your brothers were only trying to give me some light so I could finish my count. Inventory—that's what I'm hired to do." The trapper paced. With him, Nina, Alicia, and Masagawa settled themselves outside an old storefront that served as the courtroom. The building was faded, and the wood was splintered.

Some onlookers teetered over from the saloon after drinking all night. They tugged on their suspenders and tried to look dignified. Nina and her grandmother looked out of place in their Native clothes. Hoping to give testimony, the trapper had cleaned himself up for the event and left behind his rabbit fur cap and leather britches.

"You wait here." A ragged deputy directed them. He wore a torn work shirt and muddy boots. Given special authority for the day's event, he pushed the women to the side yard outside of the crumbling building. He waved the trapper toward the entry. "Not you, you can go on in." The order of admission was clear. First, White men were allowed into the makeshift courtroom. Then, the padre and novitiates, followed by the Mexican settlers—the men, that is. No women were allowed in and no tribal members, except the two men on trial.

The women had nowhere to wait. They sat outside in the dirt and passed the time. Nina's grandma strung beads and burned sage leaves in an abalone shell. She offered chants and prayers for her grandsons in her own traditional manner. Every once in a while, she murmured, "big star." Masagawa continued her private ceremony until the scrawny deputy strutted toward the trio.

"No magic around here, lady. None of your Indian spells will keep them boys from hanging," the deputy said.

25

Chapter

"Big star," Masagawa repeated.

"Why does she keep saying that?" Alicia asked Nina.

"I don't know. 'Big star' is how you say North Star—that way," Nina pointed to the north end of the pueblo. "Is that the place of the gallows?"

The trapper came out to report on the proceedings in the afternoon. He fumed at the pueblo rules and prejudices.

"Those fools won't believe me. They claim your brothers stole my weapons and burned the hides on purpose." He was red in the face and agitated. "Your friend Romo is going to ask for leniency in the sentencing. It's a fine thing since he pressed charges."

"He's only doing his job, protecting the Mission's business." Alicia felt like she should say something on Padre Romo's behalf.

"Yeah, and I'm doing mine, surveying and tracking business here," the trapper said. Alicia wanted to ask him who he worked for, but she stayed quiet.

"Brothers have no job," Nina said.

"They go big star," Masagawa repeated.

It was almost twilight when the crowd emptied the courtroom. Alicia heard a lot of muttering.

"Damned Indians ought to be run clean out of here. I don't call them braves, I call 'em thieves." Vulgar things were said in the presence of Nina and Masagawa, who were still hoping to see Pedro and Flaco released.

"Hard labor," the trapper reported to them. "They will not hang, but Romo said there's plenty of work to do in Monterey. They are being sent north to pay off their debts."

"They go," Masagawa said. Alicia realized Masagawa knew all along what the outcome would be. The brothers were being sent north to Monterey. Big star, north star.

"Is Padre Romo still in there? I need to see him." Alicia was eager to let him know about the buckets.

"Romo? The padre was right behind me. Everyone is swarming around him, mad because he was easy on the boys," the trapper said. "He's a good man."

"Padre!" Alicia called out. She could follow the top of his head in the middle of the throng. He turned from one angry man to the next, trying to calm their tempers.

"You need him, Alicia?" The trapper saw her concern. Either that, or Nina nudged him into action.

"Yes, it's pretty important to me." It was impossible for her to get the padre's attention by herself.

"Court's adjourned, men. Drinks are on me!" The trapper's voice boomed out over the cluster of angry men surrounding Padre Romo. Like a hive of bees, the complainers swarmed to the saloon. A few threw up their hats in the air and yelled, "Yahoo!" Once they were gone, Padre Romo came to stand beside the women.

"Nina, you have yourself an excellent fellow in that trapper," Padre Romo said. "He defended your brothers the best he could, and he just got me free of that angry mob." Nina blushed. Padre Romo reached out his hand toward Masagawa and helped her get to her feet. Nina collected her grandmother's beads, shells, and sage for the long trek back to the village.

"Padre, are you all right?" Alicia said. "They were so angry."

"They like to yell and argue. Jesus himself faced many an angry crowd, and I'm no match for him."

"I hate to bother you, too."

"You are no bother. What is it, my child? Tell me."

"I have a message from my sister Clara. We have more shells for the Mission." Alicia felt silly speaking in a sort of code. "Do you understand?"

"Ah, yes, shells. We can always use them." Romo searched Alicia's face to see if she was talking about what he guessed. "Are you fifteen yet?"

"Just yesterday, Padre."

"Well, well. Feliz cumpleaños, young lady." Alicia thought she saw him look her up and down. "We can certainly use those shells. When will you bring them?"

"As soon as we can. Before Tío Salvador returns to Monterey with his tax report." Could Romo understand her urgency? He looked a little confused.

"Very well, let us meet tomorrow. Until then." Romo walked away but stopped once to look back at Alicia. He still had a bewildered expression on his face.

Alicia began her walk back to the hacienda. There was still plenty of daylight. As she got near the house, she saw Clara sitting on the patio with a bucket of gold coins on either side of her chair.

"What took you so long?" Clara called out to her. "Isn't Padre Romo with you?" She didn't ask about the outcome of the trial. She was only anxious to pass on those precious buckets.

"The trial took forever; it's finally over." Alicia stepped on to the porch. "Don't you want to know what happened? Everyone was there."

"You go off to socialize while I'm here all by myself fixing lunch," Clara said.

"Socialize? You are the one who promised to walk with Tío Salvador today," Alicia said. With that exchange, Clara opened up a torrent of information.

26

Chapter

"I was so nervous, talking to Tío Salvador." Clara stood on the hacienda patio, chattering and smoothing down her skirts. "I changed my dress three times before I had the courage to come downstairs." She patted her curls, piled high. "I tied my hair back, then brushed it all out. But in the end, I decided it was best to pile it on top of my head. What do you think?"

"Why did you worry about those things?" Alicia glanced down at the pails of gold coins, hoping Clara did not share their contents with Tío Salvador, or her intention to inherit Rancho Refugio as the wife of Captain Harris.

"I didn't want him to judge me a little girl. You're the baby, not me." That was it—Clara wanted to impress Tío Salvador.

"What did he say? What did you chat about?" Alicia was afraid to ask.

"He loved the lunch I fixed! I used Mama's three best serving dishes and added hot bread with a touch of honey. He could see

Mama is dedicated to making us all good wives, but I didn't mention Harris." Alicia breathed a sigh of relief. "Not after all the mistakes Harris made, blurting out his opinions."

"What did you tell him? Did he ask you questions?" Alicia had never heard her sister criticize Captain Harris before, but now Clara recited a list of his mistakes.

"After the phony ledger book, he did nothing right. He said Nina's brothers ought to be hanged. Tío told him he did not like mean talk about the Natives. Then Harris criticized the Presidio soldiers and Tío told him what honorable men they were. He said Mexicans could run nothing but were better than the Spanish. How could Harris be so stupid? Everyone knows Tío Salvador is Spanish." Clara went on and on.

"How angry was he? Will it influence his decisions?"

"Oh no, I impressed him with my maturity. He is a man of fine character. We had a lovely conversation." Clara stopped fidgeting with her skirt and looked up at Alicia. "But what about you? You were supposed to bring Padre Romo back here so we can get rid of these buckets and settle Papa's accounts."

"Why are the buckets here? Where's Tío Salvador now?" Alicia glanced around to make sure they were alone. "Padre Romo expects us to visit him tomorrow at the Mission. What will we say to him?"

"Must we lug these buckets all the way to the Mission?" Clara said. "I don't know where Tío is. He's kind of secretive, don't you think?"

Tío Salvador walked toward the beach by himself, glad to be far away from Clara's constant chatter. Before their awkward lunch, he had a heated discussion with Captain Harris. He avoided telling Clara about the unpleasant encounter with Harris. Instead he endured her cooking and her nonstop conversation.

After lunch Salvador wanted to inspect the shell mounds on the coastline. The mounds on the beach reminded him of something, someone. It seemed like a lifetime ago that a beautiful Native woman in the north explained to him what such shell mounds signify. Without intending to, Salvador left the seashore in search of the local Native peoples. Along the way he spotted Nina and the trapper, escorting Masagawa back to her home after the trial.

"Hello there. May I bother you for an update on today's trial? How did it go for the brothers?"

"I didn't expect to meet you here. How do you guess it went? You are a man of the world." The trapper spoke to Salvador with candor.

"I've seen quick judgments handed out against Native people before. I wished for something better." Salvador wanted to sound neutral, given his official role with the governor. "Will the men serve time, or worse?"

"Time. 'Work duty in Monterey' was the court's decision," the Trapper said. "The crowd was not happy about it. The sooner those two go, the better."

"I'd like to give my condolences to their grandmother, Masagawa." Salvador said.

"I'll introduce you. Come ahead." The trapper led Salvador into Masagawa's hut.

27

Chapter

"Children bring tears." Masagawa greeted Salvador as if she knew him.

"I am so sorry to hear about the judgment against your grandsons. Perhaps I can help them in Monterey."

"You help many. Ortega girls and others," Masagawa said. "My Nina shares stories."

"We always wish to protect our children." Salvador thought of Dolores and Clara, both hurt by the same man, Captain Harris. He had not intended to discuss this with Masagawa.

Salvador's other work for the governor was to remove undesirables from the territories. This territory attracted far too many opportunists.

"I must tell Clara." Salvador asked the healer how to tell her that Harris was gone. Could he disguise Harris's banishment as a special assignment?

"Him bad man," Masagawa said. Harris's reputation along the coast as a privateer was well known to the governor and to Tío Salvador. When Salvador's relatives at Rancho Refugio reached out to him in a panic about Dolores's pregnancy, he was more than happy to tell them about the Laredo School for Young Ladies. He convinced the governor to cosign a letter of introduction and recommendation for their eldest daughter.

"Children bring tears, then make more children." Masagawa read his mind. It was a crime that Harris had pushed his way into the Ortega family. When Salvador arrived at the rancho he found that Harris had set his intentions on yet another Ortega sister. He pretended he didn't recognize the cad on that first night. Harris had established a career of breaking as many hearts as possible.

The next morning Alicia was glad to see Nina in the hacienda kitchen. Tío Salvador talked in the garden with the trapper.

"They have a lot to talk about," Alicia said. She leaned toward the window to overhear a bit of their conversation.

"He visit Masagawa," Nina said.

"What! Tío Salvador was in the village?" Alicia said.

"He visit; they talk."

"About what? Did you take him there? Why?"

"They talk brothers, Monterey, and Harris." Nina's report was accurate, but too brief for Alicia.

"Tío Salvador will make important decisions about our land. We must be careful."

"I know these things," Nina said.

"Today Clara and I will see Padre Romo. Did you know that?" Alicia said. "We've got to straighten up our affairs before Captain Harris talks to Tío Salvador again."

"He gone," Nina said.

"He's right there in the garden. What are you talking about?" Alicia was so frustrated with Nina.

"Harris gone. Tío make him go. He tell Masagawa." Alicia looked from Nina to Tío Salvador in the garden. When did all this happen? Did Clara know?

"Is there coffee?" Clara, who had risen late, came to the sala. She was dressed for the trek to the Mission. She wore a long muslin skirt, a chamois vest, and a matching bag slung over her shoulder. "Why aren't you ready to go, Alicia? It's going to be a slow walk carrying those . . . Oh, Nina! I didn't know you were here." She stopped short of mentioning of the buckets.

"Nina made coffee. Here," Alicia extended a mug to her sister. "But she's not staying long." She did not want Nina to share her news about Harris being gone.

"Well, that's just fine. We'll be at the Mission today. Leave some fruit and cheese out for Tío Salvador and Captain Harris, will you?" Clara ignored the fact that Nina was no longer working for the Ortegas. She was the trapper's woman now. "The men get hungry in the afternoon."

Alicia and Nina just stood and watched Clara drink her coffee and fuss with her hair. Tío Salvador had helped resolve the threat that Captain Harris would steal the land grant, but Alicia worried about how Clara would react when she learned he was gone. She focused on her own little world that would soon be turned upside down.

Later that same day, Padre Romo greeted Clara and Alicia in the Mission gardens.

"Welcome, young ladies. What a pleasant surprise to see both of you." He glanced around to see if anyone observed them. "What have we here?" Romo peered into the buckets and dipped his hand through the shells down toward the gold coins.

"Shells for the garden," Clara said. "We know you can always use more."

"Always," Romo said. Alicia thought their little charade was ridiculous.

"Where do you want them?" Alicia was ready to dump her bucket over on the garden path.

"No!" Romo and Clara said together. "First scrub the saltwater off. Follow us." They moved behind the chapel's side door, a spot to which coffins were wheeled before burial. Romo kept looking over his shoulder. When he was certain they were alone, he lifted the lid of a toolbox.

"Let's store the best, ah, shells here. You'll find a burlap bag at the bottom," Romo said. Alicia noticed that she and Clara did all the work. Romo never touched the shells nor the gold. The transfer completed, the buckets were discarded. A young novitiate approached with a tray of tea and cakes.

"Tea, Padre?" The novitiate set a small table for the threesome. They sat with an unobstructed view of the toolbox holding their secrets.

28

Chapter

"The Lord giveth," Padre Romo said. He dusted sugar from the cakes off his lips and smiled at the two Ortega sisters. "That's all, thank you." Padre Romo excused the young man serving. "So, ladies, who is the fortunate recipient of the mysterious Ortega legacy today?" Romo was cautious. He could be overheard, and yet not understood, by anyone.

"It's a general gift for the pueblo, Padre." Clara spoke in a loud voice. She used the wording they decided would be best.

"All those, ah, shells for a general gift? I'm not sure I understand," Padre Romo said.

"It's an enormous gift. Many haciendas pay that amount in taxes each year." Clara went on. "That would be one way to record it."

"In the tax register?" Padre Romo sat at attention. "For that I would need the help of a special clerk."

"We know you can have it recorded in the Ortega tax columns to cover past due taxes." Clara gave direction to the padre. Alicia felt a bit of pride in her sister.

"If there's any left, share it with the Native village," said Alicia. "What do you think?" Clara didn't agree, though Alicia thought it fair.

"Use the extra for the needs at the Mission," Clara said.

"Ah, well, this is an uncommon request indeed." Was the padre surprised, or just playing along? Alicia made sure their message was clear.

"It clears the entire Ortega deed to our land," she said.

"I'm sure the padre knows best how to do his work." Clara assumed the land would be a part of her dowry when she married Captain Harris. Did she envision her wedding ceremony inside the Mission sanctuary?

As they walked back to the hacienda, the sisters giggled over their exchange with Padre Romo. Leaving their buckets behind made the journey home easy. The two Ortega girls had settled an old debt, one that was incurred before either of them was born. Their parents would be proud.

"Did you notice how nervous he was?" Alicia said. "I thought he would faint when the boy brought tea into the garden."

"You must admit, you've learned a lot from your older sister." Clara took credit for the plan to the clear the Ortega taxes. She expected it to be to her direct benefit as an heir.

"I've learned from both of you." Learned what not to do, Alicia thought. "It won't be long now; Mama and Papa will return. Won't they be surprised?"

"I'll have to wait until their return to make our wedding arrangements," Clara said. "Now that the taxes are clear, I can think clearly about marriage plans. Have you seen Captain Harris?"

"Not at the trial or the hacienda." Alicia tried to sound casual, not sharing the news of his departure. She almost felt sorry for her sister.

"No matter. I can get more done when he's not around. That's the way men are. Ha, another free lesson from your big sister."

"Why marry in the first place?" This was Alicia's genuine feeling, observing Mama follow Papa to Laredo, Nina serving the trapper, Dolores sent away because of Harris, and now Clara preferring to make plans on her own.

"You'll learn."

29

Chapter

Back at the hacienda, they changed their dusty skirts. The morning's walk exhausted them. They nibbled on fruit and cheese and lay down to an afternoon siesta. When they awoke, Tío Salvador leaned over the table sorting documents and sketches from his work in Monterey. Papa's brandy bottle was opened on a side table and three small glasses lay nearby.

"Good evening, ladies. Did you have a good rest?"

"Tío?" Both girls were still groggy from their sleep.

"What is this?" Alicia saw his sketches on the table. "Is it Monterey? Just look at these drawings!"

"It will be grander by the time I return," Tío said. "I have been sorting my papers all day. Where did you two spend your day?"

"I would love to see this place, Monterey. Are any of those buildings shops?" Clara hovered over the drawings.

"There are many shops and merchants. Would you like to see it?" He said. "These sketches are government buildings. Here's the Mission. You realize we are an important territory. So important that the United States has its eye on acquiring the land."

"But we are Mexicans, not Americans," Alicia said. "The States are so far away. Could such a change happen? What would become of us?"

"We should ask Nina's trapper. He told me about the Yankees and their agents here in the territory. He is one of them," Tío said.

"You cannot trust a White man who chooses a Native wife, like Nina," Clara said.

"Clara! Nina was given to him by her brothers. And besides, she is our friend," Alicia said.

"She may be your so-called friend, but she is our household servant, nothing more." Clara's mean spirit filled the room. "I'll go find us some bread and honey," Clara muttered and left the sala.

"You must excuse my sister; she is overexcited with the events."

"Yes, of course, with recent events," Salvador finished Alicia's sentence. "Perhaps you can give us some time alone when she returns." Now he would tell Clara that Captain Harris was gone. Alicia wished she could be present to watch Clara react, but another part of her felt bad for the pain she would endure.

"Will you tell her?" Alicia said. "I know the secrets you shared with Masagawa. Nina told me."

"It's best if you do not share that. Leave me alone with Clara."

Alicia left the sala but remained within earshot. Tío spoke in a low voice and Clara continued to chatter about the shops in Monterey. The conversation got lower and slower. Tío Salvador was gentle with his news. Alicia heard him say, "He left this for

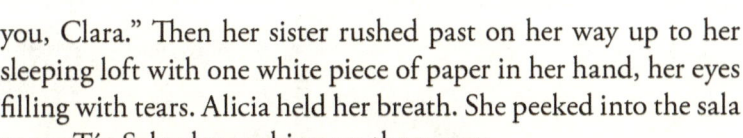

you, Clara." Then her sister rushed past on her way up to her sleeping loft with one white piece of paper in her hand, her eyes filling with tears. Alicia held her breath. She peeked into the sala to see Tío Salvador packing up the papers.

"You can come back, Alicia. Your sister is going to need your help in the next few days. Who knows, you may hear from your mama and papa soon."

"What did you tell her?"

"I think I should leave that for Clara to tell you herself. In the morning I go to discuss affairs with the tax collector. After that, my official business is done."

"We will miss you, Tío, and be lonely without you."

"There is another thing you should know. Nina and the trapper are going to accompany Pedro and Flaco up to Monterey in the same convoy that takes me back to the capital."

"That cannot be true. Nina would have told me," Alicia said.

30

Chapter

"Can you make Nina stay?" Alicia's problems overwhelmed her—how distant she and Nina had become since Dolores left and the trapper appeared. It had been months since her parents went to Laredo. Now the challenge of losing her best friend made her want to cry.

"Nina is free to go where she wishes now, Alicia. When we grow older, life changes. I'm so sorry you will miss her," Tío Salvador said. "It is time for your parents to be here. Remember, they are bringing home a new baby. They will need your help."

Alicia could not keep herself from worrying about her next problem. She knew she should be happy that her parents would soon return, but what would it be like to have an infant in their home? Life would not be the same. She sipped coffee with Tío Salvador in silence. Clara did not come down for breakfast.

"I'll be on my way to the tax collector's office. He opens early," Tío Salvador said.

"Are you sure I cannot go with you?"

"No, you stay here and watch for Clara. She's got to come downstairs sometime." Tío Salvador gathered his bag filled with official records and land grant documents. He glanced up the landing toward Clara's sleeping loft. There was no sign of her.

"I'll be here for her, don't worry. You don't think she will do anything desperate, do you?" Alicia knew her sister felt abandoned by the departure of Captain Harris.

"I'm sure Harris used his letter to put the best slant on his sudden departure." Tío Salvador moved toward the patio. "Whatever she says, just go along with it." He started down the pathway toward the pueblo.

Alicia guessed Tío didn't tell Clara the absolute truth about Captain Harris. Padre Romo did not give the tax collector the absolute truth about the taxes. Mama and Papa never told the truth about the Spanish gold hidden in their cave. Was this what grownups were like? Her sisters were already starting down a path of half-truths.

On the dock, the Mexican flag hung from the pole where Harris had left it. Alicia walked toward it, hoping to be cheered by the tidy dock, the familiar ropes and baskets she had played with since her childhood. She recalled times with Papa on the dock. He loved to tell her stories and show her how to mend nets and tie knots. Now she questioned all the stories he told. She wondered about the genuine history of her family. It was the first time she felt unhappy on the dock. She rushed back to the house.

Clara was sitting in the sala when Alicia entered the hacienda. Her hair was loose and tangled. She wore an old bathrobe and heavy socks. Clara stared at a paper that lay in her lap. It was Captain Harris's letter. Her eyes were still red after crying all night.

"Clara. You're up. Let me serve you coffee." Alicia hated to see her sister so defeated.

"I guess you know the wedding plans will have to wait. Have you been laughing at me?"

"Here, take this." Alicia handed over a warm mug. "No, I'm not laughing. I care about you."

"Where have I heard that before? Believe nothing a man tells you, little sister. Where is Tío Salvador? I've never been so embarrassed in my life."

"He went to the tax clerk. You and I should be happy, today of all days. We did what was right. You were smart to take the buckets to Padre Romo."

"That's a laugh. Now everything is wrong." Clara covered her face with her hands, crushing Harris's letter against her cheek. "Tío gave him a commission, he ruined my life."

"What?" Alicia was shocked, then remembered, "The kindest thing you can do is go along with her story."

"Tío Salvador told Harris about an emergency in the Philippines. He needed a new commissioner for their docks. Harris jumped at the chance as soon as he heard." Clara's eyes filled with tears. "He never even thought of me."

"I'm sure he didn't mean to hurt you."

"Not Tío, he tried to stop him. It was Harris who insisted on taking the commission." Clara bowed her head. Alicia tried to make sense of her story. Why give a commission to an American like Harris? She decided it was best to keep quiet.

"He left a letter and didn't bother to say goodbye, the coward. Poor Tío had to make his apologies last night. I didn't want to cry in front of him." Clara clenched her fists. "I can't believe that this has happened to me."

"Tío has been kind to us, all of us. Who would have expected it?"

"It could be years." Clara gulped for breath as she cried out loud. "Does he think I'm going to wait?" Her expression turned to anger. "Who cares about the Philippines?"

31

Chapter

The sisters spent the rest of the day together. Alicia tried to give Clara extra attention. She brushed out her hair and complimented her on the clothes she picked out to wear. It was near sunset when Clara pulled herself together enough to get dressed. They fixed omelets with green chilies for a simple dinner.

"I think we are old enough to help ourselves to Papa's brandy, don't you?" Clara's suggestion shocked Alicia, but she was going along with whatever her sister proposed.

"Here's to the Ortega sisters who saved the rancho!" They toasted one another. What a bitter taste. That brandy was worse than medicine. Alicia let it dribble out of her mouth onto a napkin.

"Papa runs this place, sure." Clara waved her arms as she spoke. "But why do we need a man?" They laughed even though they were uncertain of the future.

"What do you think will happen when Mama brings home Dolores's baby?"

"Shhh, don't say that!" Clara slurred her words. "Remember, it's Mama's baby. Papa said so, Padre Romo agrees, and we better go along."

"I've never been around a baby. How was it when I was little?"

"We were just a few years apart," Clara wagged her finger in the air. "But Mama and Papa were younger in those days."

"I know nothing about babies, do you?" Alicia capped the brandy and put it back in the cupboard.

"Nina will do all that work. We won't be expected to do that sort of thing." Clara finished her omelet and searched for any remaining strawberries.

"I guess you are right. Women have help with their babies all the time, right?" Eventually Alicia would share the news about Nina leaving for Monterey. But not tonight, when she and Clara could laugh together and be sisters.

Alicia did not want to face the next morning. She stayed curled up close to the fireplace, clutching Mama's shawl until she heard others waking in the house. It would be a day of goodbyes. Farewell to Tío Salvador who returned to Monterey, adiós to Nina who followed the path of the trapper, and goodbye to Nina's brothers, Pedro and Flaco, sentenced to hard labor in Monterey. Alicia didn't care about the brothers, who she blamed for trading their sister as if she were a goat or a cow.

"Who is this sleepyhead?" Tío Salvador placed his belongings by the door. He drew a large envelope from his satchel.

"Oh dear, so sorry I slept in." Alicia stretched and gathered up the shawl. "When did you return from the pueblo?"

"I was late and didn't want to wake you. Here is something special I brought." He handed over the large envelope sealed with wax and tied with a ribbon the colors of the Mexican flag.

"For me? What is it? It looks important."

"It's for your papa. Can you keep this safe until he returns? It is private."

"Is it—" Alicia's question was interrupted when Clara entered the sala.

"Whispering? What's going on? Why are your bags packed?" Clara liked to turn everything into a mystery. The three of them shared coffee and pan tostado. Alicia packed a bag of fruit and cheese for Tío's trip.

"For you, and one for Nina." Alicia handed Tío an extra bag. Too late, she realized she should not have mentioned Nina.

"Where is that girl? Why are we fixing our own coffee and toast?" Clara said.

"We will see her at the pueblo today. Her brothers are also leaving with the convoy to Monterey," Alicia said.

"They get to travel? I thought they were in jail."

"They will be prisoners in Monterey doing hard labor," Tío Salvador explained.

"Good riddance to them." Once again, half-truths and harsh judgments filled the conversation in the Ortega household, Alicia thought. This time she was the one withholding the truth of Nina's departure. Now she had an extra responsibility to hide the big official envelope for Papa's return.

A crowd of curious onlookers gathered at the jail as Nina's brothers were brought out.

"Good riddance. Out with the trash," the crowd jeered when Pedro and Flaco appeared. The prisoners' bound ankles and wrists made it awkward for them to get on the wagon.

"Stand back, let them through." One guard took special care to shelter the brothers from the angry crowd. The men were tied to the wagon to keep them from escaping along the way.

"*Provecho*, provisions." Alicia noticed that this same young guard, a man she had never seen before today, slipped them bread and water for their journey. The wagon was just one part of the official convoy, escorted by Presidio soldiers. Tío Salvador's carriage, pulled by four horses, took the lead spot. Other soldiers, workers, and that young novitiate from the Mission had donkeys to ride. Some folks from the pueblo walked behind the entourage. Alicia spotted Nina and the trapper among the walkers.

Nina, Nina. She willed Nina to look her way. Waving away years of friendship seemed feeble. Alicia forgot to bring a gift or a token for Nina beyond the bag of fruit and cheese she asked Tío to share. The trapper looked bigger than ever, standing among all the Native people. Now that Alicia knew he was an agent for the United States government, she trusted him even less than before. Nina looked like a child next to him, her head barely reaching his shoulder. He was staring at Alicia and pointing his large staff in her direction as he leaned down to speak.

Nina broke away from the crowd and approached Alicia. Was she changing her mind? Did the trapper give her permission to remain at the Ortega hacienda? Alicia wanted to grab her friend and drag her back into the days of their childhood. But Nina stood stiffly in front of her. When she looked up, her eyes were brimming with tears. The girls struggled to speak; their throats were so tight with suppressed sobs.

"I did not bring you anything," Alicia whispered.

"Visit Masagawa. She alone now." Nina pressed Alicia's palm to her rounded belly.

"Girls, they are leaving!" Padre Romo called out to Alicia and Nina. He stood nearby with a boy at his side. Nina rushed back to the trapper and the long line of travelers.

"Nina!" Alicia sobbed a goodbye.

"She will make a new home and family." Padre Romo approached and put a hand on Alicia's shoulder. "Be happy for her."

32

Chapter

nlike her sisters, Alicia liked to wear grubby work clothes. It made her feel ready for action, more determined, and more resourceful. She dug into the clothes basket and reached for her dungarees and ragged dock shirt. She was overjoyed to be back in the quiet of her home after her sad goodbyes with friends departing for Monterey. A knit cap lay nearby. She snatched it and tucked her long hair underneath.

"Two ships are arriving." She found Clara pulling weeds that grew up between the beans and onions in Mama's garden and announced her news. Sitting in the dirt, wearing a broad floppy hat, Clara looked like Mama.

"The Presidio scouts spotted them on the horizon," Alicia reported. "One is headed to the government port; the other may anchor here." They both had chores at the hacienda now, since they were alone. Clara tended the yard and the hens. Alicia tended the anchorage, like Papa used to do.

"They might as well sail on. Papa's not here." Clara shook soil off an onion.

"I will handle it. If Papa, Tío Salvador, and Harris are all gone, then I'll work at the tie-up."

"By yourself? You're just a girl." Clara rubbed a hand on her back and straightened up. "I'll pull weeds, but I can't plant and plan like Mama, or cook and clean like Nina."

"We must until they come home. Where is Harris's ledger? I have an idea." The sisters went inside to rummage through the sala for the homemade accounts book.

"Look, it still has empty pages. I'll make a list of the ships, captains, dates, and merchandise here." Alicia tore out some of the stiff pages and got Papa's quill and pen. "Help me calculate the real tax so we never fall behind again."

"But will the men pay us? I could never ask a strange fellow for money."

"We'll write an invoice and place their payments in the ledger. It's the family dock and we are Ortegas, the only Ortegas here now."

Alicia waited for the ship to approach all afternoon. She strolled back and forth and heard the shell mound below the planks crunch and clack. She wondered if Nina's relatives were complaining about her disturbance above. A dinghy filled with goods approached.

"Ahoy. Hola," a sailor called. "Señor Ortega?"

"Bienvenido, welcome." Alicia threw out a line, the same way she'd seen her papa do many times. "Tie up."

"Where is señor Ortega? We want to off-load our goods and continue moving on!"

"I am Ortega, move on through." The sailor looked over the tall skinny youth in work clothes and a cap.

"Okay, Ortega, tow the line before I pull you in the water!"

"I have it." A youngster, about twelve, surprised Alicia when he ran toward the line and pulled with all his might. Surprised, she asked, "Who are you and where did you come from?"

"God be with you and your ship, sailor." Padre Romo strode up to the boat tie-up, ready to lend authority. Then Alicia remembered seeing that same young boy with Romo earlier in the morning in the pueblo. The padre winked at Alicia and peered into the approaching dinghy.

"Thank you, Padre." The sailor handed bundled goods to the boy and Alicia. Behind the first dinghy were three more, all full of new stock to off-load. Alicia lifted the ledger out of a crate and opened a new page.

"Vessel name? Captain's name? Last dock?" She fired questions at the bewildered sailor and recorded his replies. The boy scrambled among the piles of cargo, calling out the goods.

"But where is the regular man, Padre? Is he ill?" The sailor ignored Alicia.

"He is well, and this is the Ortega dock, sailor," Romo said.

"This is the Ortega invoice." Alicia handed the sheet to the padre, too afraid to give it to the sailor.

"Everything in order here. Ortega needs your mark on it." Romo passed the invoice to a sailor who looked at them in disbelief.

"My captain signs this." He rowed back to the ship without complaint. When he was out of earshot, Alicia pulled the cap off her head and her curls tumbled down around her shoulders.

"How did you know I needed help?"

"The dock is a busy place, and young Roberto needs some practice. We hoped you might employ him for the price of a hot lunch."

"Lunch and more. Your help is most welcome here, Roberto. Let's go see what my sister has prepared for our meal."

"Roberto's papa is an officer with many children to feed. A warm lunch and a peek at the new goods will give us energy," Romo said.

33

Chapter

"What's wrong with vegetables? They are good for us, fresh and, ah, that's all there is today!" Clara struggled to come up with a decent lunch. She used what she collected in the garden. "What can I do here all alone? Then you bring unannounced guests."

"It's fine, Clara." Alicia tried to soothe her sister's frayed nerves.

"This looks delicious, Clara. I brought almonds to share." Padre Romo and Roberto settled around the table to join the sisters for lunch.

"Clara, you should have seen the expression on that sailor's face when we handed him an invoice for his docking privileges." Alicia was proud of the morning's accomplishments and thankful for her helpers. "The old ledger worked." She didn't want her sister to give up so soon. They needed to keep the hacienda running until Mama and Papa returned.

"Okay, you manage the dock, but I'm not prepared to run the house like Mama did. Do you expect me to be the gardener, and cook, and cleaner?" Clara was near tears.

"Several girls at the Mission are ready to go to work. Why don't I assign you someone to help?" Romo could see Clara's frustration. "Roberto, you return to help Alicia. I'll send someone with you to help Clara."

"I want Nina back. Make her come back, Padre. She already knows all our routines."

"Nina has begun her own household, free from Mission service."

"She is making a family with that trapper? He's a White man and he can't have her!" Clara said.

"She is his wife and having a baby." Alicia had trouble saying the words.

"What? She is still a girl. She cannot do that."

"A new helper will ease your burdens. Trust me." While Romo talked, Roberto ate vegetables. It had been a long time since he had been able to eat his fill.

"You were ready to marry Captain Harris and girls my age have children every day. Let's take Padre Romo's generous offer. Have some more squash before Roberto finishes it." They all laughed at their plates full of vegetables and almonds. "I'll help make eggs for dinner."

The next day Roberto returned with a helper, a young Chumash girl who was too shy to come into the hacienda.

"It's about time. There's plenty to be done." Clara barked orders that made the Native girl even more withdrawn.

"Show her the garden," Alicia suggested. "She may not have been in a proper house before." Alicia showed the frightened girl where to shell peas out near the cooking ramada. "Roberto and

I will coil the ropes this morning. I'm expecting our first signed invoice. Isn't it exciting?"

"I'm going to take a walk. Maybe I'll collect some flowers." Clara's voice was dull and glum.

By midday Alicia and Roberto returned to the sala hoping to find a hot lunch.

"Get the plates! Can you do anything?" Clara screamed. Bread and fresh butter lay in the middle of the table next to a pot of droopy flowers. The new girl peered in from the patio, too afraid to enter the house.

"Clara, you are frightening her." Alicia watched Roberto smear thick butter on his bread and wondered if he might try to eat the flowers.

"She's supposed to help. At least get us water." Clara flung a bucket at the poor girl. She seemed glad to escape the house and walk toward the stream.

"Roberto learned some new words today. I showed him on the ledger." Alicia buttered her bread and downed it.

"This is not working, Alicia. That girl must go back." Clara tried to perk up the wilted flowers. "I never guessed I'd miss Nina so much." Alicia thought the same thing to herself. She missed Nina more than she could have imagined. At least Roberto was someone to support her with simple tasks, and she enjoyed teaching him. She watched as the new helper walked away.

When the next ship approached the dock, the young crew, Alicia and Roberto, were ready with their cables and the ledger. This time the sailors did not hesitate to interact with the new Ortega team. By noon the cargo was stored and a signed invoice delivered back to Alicia. She was ecstatic.

"Another invoice! Clara, where are you?" Alicia had worked up an enormous appetite. The table in the sala was empty. A tremendous squawking came from the hen house. Clara was running after the chickens and swinging a knife like a mad-woman. Roberto doubled over with laughter.

"Hush, Roberto, she'll hear you!"

"Leave it to me. Make a fire, boil some water. That's what my mama does." Roberto walked toward Clara and took the knife from her hand. In one moved he grabbed a plump chicken by the neck, swung it over his head, and the squawking stopped.

"That's remarkable. Awful, but remarkable," Clara said. "Let's cook some corn, too." After an hour's preparation, they feasted on chicken and corn. Not one scrap was left on their plates.

"Can you bring your mama with you tomorrow, Roberto?" Clara had been thinking up a plan. "We need an experienced woman to run this house like Mama used to do."

"But she is an officer's wife and has her own family to care for," Alicia said.

"My mama will come. We need the money; that is why I am here." Roberto spoke with no shame.

"Good. It's settled." Clara pulled a chicken leg apart with her bare hands.

34

Chapter

Roberto's mama, Maria Rodriguez, arrived at the Ortega hacienda the next day, and her six children accompanied her.

"What's all this?" Clara blurted out, instead of the traditional welcome. "This is not a nursery." She invariably said the wrong thing.

"This is my household, *señorita*. My son Roberto tells me you are having problems taking care of yours. Where is your family?" Maria would not be cowed by privileged girls. She had met many such women among the officers' wives.

Maria had married a low-level military officer at the Presidio in Alta California. They were allowed a family subsidy, but the extra financial support was delayed through the slow processes of the Mexican bureaucracy. The family lived in a tiny house beside the garrison with a garden plot that Maria tended.

"Hello, I am Alicia. Your son Roberto is so helpful. You have trained him well."

"I've raised him to work, as we all must do." Maria glanced around the veranda, then the sala, and the garden. She was not timid like the Mission girls who did housekeeping. "Let us begin then. The sun waits for no one."

"But—" Clara was no match for her.

"Lupita, take the baby to the garden," Maria directed her eldest daughter, who held an infant on her hip.

"Sí, Mama." Lupita looked younger than Alicia.

"Roberto, su hermano David, *afuera*." She directed him to get his brother outside. Both boys would join Alicia on the wharf today. The sisters stood aside and watched this woman, Maria, take charge.

"*Chata, conmigo*." A chubby shy daughter, perhaps a twin to Lupita, tagged along with her mother to the cooking ramada. The Ortega home was invaded by the Rodriguez army and offered scant resistance.

"Wait for me." Alicia reached for the ledger and followed Roberto and his brother to the tie-up. Clara quietly disappeared to her sleeping loft upstairs and peeked down every so often.

The Ortega crew was prepared, but no ships docked that day. Alicia spent most of her time watching the boys play. They assembled the baskets and disassembled them just as she had done as a toddler. As the youngest in her family, she never spent time with small children. What would the new Ortega baby be like? She did not know if it was a boy or a girl. That news was less important to her now that Harris was gone. All the old taxes were paid, and the land grant was secure.

By noon, the three of them walked toward the house. Steps away, the savory aromas and sound of laughter made it seem like someone else's home. Maria Rodriguez and her family worked their magic on the property. Everything was orderly and the table full of food for the noon meal. The only person missing was Clara.

"Provecho, enjoy your meal by the grace of God." Maria offered a prayer over the meal. Although the Ortegas had long since given up saying a grace before they ate, there was much to be grateful for. Midway through lunch, Clara slipped in and quietly took a place at the table.

Maria's children reached from plate to mouth as the elders helped the younger siblings scoop their soup and cut their vegetables. They made many silly jokes, thanking the chicken and the squash and the corn individually. Clara sat with her lips tight and her hands in her lap.

No one stood until they spotted a fellow at the door. It was the same officer who tended to Nina's brothers when they departed.

"Señora Rodriguez, assemble the children." The youthful officer saluted.

"Hola, Manuel, do you know these two ladies?" Maria spoke with a sly note in her voice. "This splendid property belongs to their fortunate papa." Alicia blushed.

The young man was so handsome she forgave Maria immediately. Then she realized how ridiculous she appeared in her dock clothes. The dungarees were smudged, her shirt wrinkled, and her hair was still tucked up in a knit cap.

"Ladies, this is my husband's assistant, Private Valdez."

"Your carriage awaits." Manuel Valdez did not look at the sisters or their expensive house but scooped up the two youngest children and burbled nonsense words to them.

"You are leaving so soon!" Clara held out her hand as if she could hold the full group back. "What about our dinner tonight?" Everyone grew quiet and peered at her.

"My husband also demands his dinner. He wants to see his 'nursery,' as you call it. Lupita packed up plates for you and your sister to enjoy tonight. Our part is done here." The children recognized the sternness in their mother's voice and remained silent. The lovely day was falling into an argument. Then Private Valdez spoke up and added to the tensions.

35

Chapter

"I am required to collect your dock receipts for the monthly accounting," Private Valdez said.

"My receipts? Those are our private accounts. Who requires this?" When Alicia spoke, Manuel looked directly at her, inspecting her dungarees and boots.

"Excuse me, miss?" The youngster snickered. "The tax clerk collects them routinely. It is regulation."

"Well, he can't have them." Alicia was uncomfortable under Manuel's gaze.

"I am happy to come back tomorrow to give you a chance to create copies," Manuel said.

"Yes, tomorrow. We always report up to the minute. Right?" Clara gave a gold coin to Maria Rodriguez. "We thank you for your work in our home today. Please return." The tension broke and the children piled into the old wagon with Private Valdez.

"Until tomorrow," he said and turned to leave.

The next morning Alicia copied the original dock receipts and thought about the business of Rancho Refugio. Maria freshened Mother Mary's shelf. The saint looked very content among new candles on Mama's altar. Roberto, ready for his dock job, swept up the patio while he waited.

"Clara, do we have enough gold to cover new taxes on these shipments?"

"Don't you know anything about business? You trade the goods collected on the tie-up to generate a profit and then pay taxes," Clara said.

"But who do we sell to?" Alicia never thought through the entire process. A great business mind she turned out to be.

"Roberto can take goods to the pueblo with him. He'll know how to peddle them." Clara sounded so confident in her answers. "Load up some bigger things for Private Valdez. After he gathers the papers, he can trade among the other soldiers."

"But they don't work for us. This is my responsibility." Alicia regretted her ignorance about running the dock.

"They won't work for free; each person who sells takes a slight profit. That's how Papa did it. Even Padre Romo sold for Papa."

"The padre? Did he keep a profit?" Alicia continued to be surprised by how grown-ups acted.

"He would claim he donated the profits to a certain Mission fund, I'm sure." Clara stood by the front door, a hat shading her face, heavy gloves covering her hands. "Come on, I'll go with you to pick out a few choice items."

The sisters moved to the dock; Roberto followed close behind. The rest of the morning was spent rummaging through the crates and boxes collected from the ship cargoes of the previous days. Blankets, shoes, teapots, knives, dried fruits and nuts, parchments and parasols. They amassed an inventory to sell off and set aside the rest to store in a dry place before the rains came.

"We could start a market with all this." Alicia's records did not begin to account for all the cargo.

"A shop? Where? Would you want shoppers tramping through our residence? Papa always said, 'Keep it moving. The ships bring it in and we move it out.' That's how it works, sister."

"Okay then, let's get Papa's buckboard here and fill it up. Roberto, how many stops can you and I make between here and the pueblo?" She lined up crates of odds and ends. "Is this Wednesday? This will be 'fruit and nuts' day. Let's protect anything that might be ruined by sitting too long."

That first wagonload of merchandise traded in no time. Alicia looked forward to Private Valdez's visits to collect invoices for the tax clerk so she could off-load more goods with him. The days at the rancho were busy and productive. Maria Rodriguez returned with her family every day and made repairs, improvements, and wonderful meals. Ships kept docking, Alicia kept the records, and the cargoes moved to market.

The challenge of running the dock and maintaining the hacienda was finally met with Maria's help. Now Alicia had to face a new problem; she had completely forgotten her promise to Nina to visit Masagawa in the Native village. She had to make arrangements for the visit and felt guilty about putting it off for such a long time.

36

Chapter

"Be careful, you shouldn't go to that village alone." Clara's words were muffled. She helped Maria with a sewing project and held extra hooks and pins in her mouth.

"I'll be back before twilight." Alicia noticed her sister picking up a lot of motherly mannerisms, the longer she worked with Maria Rodriguez. "Good luck with the curtains." Alicia was no longer a baby. She could visit Masagawa all by herself.

Near the village, Alicia expected to hear the Native children playing by the stream or among the trees. She noticed very little noise besides the birds and breeze in the oaks. The creak of a wooden wagon startled her.

"Alicia Ortega, is that you?" Private Valdez, used to seeing Alicia in her grubby dock clothes, did not recognize her. Her beauty surprised him.

"Private, you gave me a fright." Alicia noticed a rifle and a shovel in the back of his wagon. "I'm visiting my friend's grandma. Everything seems so silent here. What are you doing here?" Valdez looked at the Native land he had been ordered to clear, then back at Alicia.

"I think you are in the wrong spot. There's no one out here."

"You're new to our territory, Private. I've lived here all my life and I'm telling you there's a friend, a healer by the name of Masagawa, who lives here." Alicia sped up her steps. He may be handsome, but he was not very smart.

"Señorita Ortega, stop. There is no village here, not anymore." Manuel got down from his wagon and caught up with Alicia. "I've been here all week on cleanup duty." He gently broke his news. "I know you are talking about the old woman."

"Her name is Masagawa. She's a healer, I tell you!" Alicia's patience grew thin.

"But she's the one whose grandsons burned the Mission. They were tried and sent off to do hard labor in Monterey. Right?"

"It was all a mistake." Alicia stared at him in disbelief. "Where is she? Is she okay?" Then she realized what he'd said, and why he carried a rifle and shovel. "Cleanup duty? What is that?"

"Just calm down. I'm sure she's fine. She left with the rest of them. The Mission is going to cultivate this space. They need the land." Valdez noticed Alicia did not appear so attractive when she became angry.

"This is their land. Where have they gone?" Alicia tried to look beyond the bushes toward the spot where Masagawa's hut stood on her last visit.

"They set up in the next valley over near the creek. Let me show you where. I'm happy to take you." What could he answer to make amends? He was only doing his duty.

"Don't show me anything." She had looked forward to seeing Valdez each time he collected invoices. "How could you be a part of clearing them out of their homes?" Alicia cursed herself for delaying her visit. She could have prevented this or talked Padre Romo out of it. "Don't you ever bother coming back to our rancho. From now on, I'll send in our dock invoices with Roberto."

Alicia set out to find Masagawa by herself. She fumed with disappointment about Manuel Valdez, the first man she ever found attractive. He was a coldhearted coward. She stomped toward the valley and the creek.

Clara was right—she shouldn't have gone alone. It was dark and cold by the time Alicia got to the relocated village. She had no shawl and no torch light, just a stubborn determination to fulfill her promise to Nina. The sweet scents coming from a makeshift shelter were Masagawa's healing herbs.

"Hello, it's me, Alicia. May I come in?" She peered around a blanket hanging from a shrub. Masagawa sat fanning a small flame. She looked the same as the last time they met. She gestured with one hand for Alicia to sit with her.

"Valdez?" Masagawa said with the slightest smile on her lips.

"Don't mention that man's name! I can't believe what he did to you." Alicia could not hold back her anger. The old woman now had to live in this tiny space. "Valdez is cruel and stupid. I am so sorry I did not come sooner."

"You come to court, you good." Masagawa remembered Alicia and Nina waiting with her while her grandsons stood trial. "Valdez carry pots and herbs. He good man." How could Masagawa think that? How could she forgive him for clearing her people out of their village?

"He is not good! That is your land."

"Tea?" Masagawa held out a small gourd with steaming liquid. "He pretty, too."

"Men are not pretty. Especially not that man." Alicia sipped the calming tea.

"Nina have powerful trapper." Masagawa knew what went on around her. "They go be near brothers and make a baby. Big north." As she spoke the hut's blanketed entry began to flutter and someone drew back the covering.

37

Chapter

"You all right?" someone whispered in Masagawa's space.

"Tea." Masagawa held up another gourd.

Alicia noticed she used only one hand. Her other lay limp in her lap. Valdez came in and took the tea as if he was an old friend of the healer.

"What are you doing here? Did you follow me?"

"It's dark, it's cold; you can't walk home alone," Valdez said.

"Good man," Masagawa repeated. "You go with him. I bless you and the baba." Alicia couldn't believe Masagawa's friendly manner toward Valdez. She was old, maybe confused, but somehow she remembered the baby coming home with Mama and Papa.

"What baba is she talking about?" Valdez blushed.

"Don't you worry about it. Thank you for your blessing, Masagawa."

"Take." The healer held up her sage bundle and Alicia remembered Nina's story about the sage blessings.

Alicia did not expect to return home in a wagon next to Private Manuel Valdez that night. He reached under the seat, drew out an old blanket and handed it to her. She wrapped it around her shoulders like a barrier between herself and the young man. It felt safe to be covered on the chilly star-filled night.

"Orion—see the three stars hang from his belt?" Valdez tried to start a conversation. "Over there, the Little Dipper. Makes me think of Masagawa's hot tea."

"She said you were good. I still can't believe what you did to her village."

"Why can't you understand? I had a job to complete. They are safe, near a stream. She told me you would be a fine woman someday."

"You and I can't decide where they will live. This is their homeland."

"I never get to decide anything. I work for a living."

"Let's not talk; do you mind?" Alicia hated the thought that anyone, even Masagawa, would give opinions about her to Private Valdez. Why would she do that?

A rut in the road bumped the wagon back and forth. Alicia's shoulder bumped against Valdez. She pulled away. What did he mean he worked for a living? Wasn't she working at the dock, collecting invoices, paying taxes?

"I work. No one makes me do things that will hurt others." Then another bump, another brush with his shoulder. "I work hard for our rancho." The wagon ride could have been romantic, but Alicia wanted to get away from Valdez.

"I've seen your invoices. I haven't told you, but the tax clerk laughs at them. Someday you may learn what actual work is."

"How dare you! Let me out of this wagon." Alicia scooted to the edge of the seat and felt Valdez's firm grip on her arm.

"I apologize. Calm down and stay put. Truth is, I'm a little jealous of you and your sister, all that land, that big house on the hill overlooking the Pacific, and your own dock."

"Jealous? It's our family's land. My parents have been through a lot." She wanted to tell Valdez about the shipwreck, the gold, Dolores's baby, everything. She pressed her lips together.

"Alicia, work is what you do when your family is hungry and has no land, or dock, or garden. You must follow orders. You can't choose who you will work for." He tugged back on the reins and faced her. "Sometimes you have to do things you realize are wrong, like moving others out of their homes."

"But you did it."

"I did it, then checked to be sure Masagawa was all right. I earn my dinner at the Presidio and a bunk under a roof. It's my work." Valdez flicked the rein on the horse. Alicia had no response. She could not forget the buckets of Ortega gold or her fear of life without the rancho.

"Well, next time, I'm going with you to deliver the invoices. If that old clerk thinks they are so funny, maybe he can give me a proper sample. I can learn."

When Alicia and Private Valdez arrived at the house, candles burned in every window. The front door burst open, and the Rodriguez children came running out.

"Manuel!" the children called out. Maria Rodriguez walked out, supporting Clara's arm. The women grew close, working together in the house. Was something wrong?

"We were so worried. It's late. Where have you been?"

"We are fine. What are the children still doing here?" Alicia said.

"Maria would not leave me alone until you returned. We didn't know that Manuel was with you." Clara spoke with unmasked suspicion.

"They are here now, and our friend Manuel can take us all home." Maria's voice calmed the scene and, as always, she made perfect sense. "Share your news with Alicia when the little ones are gone."

"News? Is everything okay?" Alicia felt a moment of panic.

"Everything is fine, except we have many sleepyheads to get to bed." Maria said. "Say goodnight to the Ortega sisters, children."

As Alicia got out of Private Valdez's wagon, the children piled in, ready for their ride back to the Presidio. She did not look forward to explaining her visit to Clara. It turned out that Clara's news would be their topic of conversation: a letter from Dolores. Clara read it out loud.

38

Chapter

Dear Sisters,

So much time has passed. I received no letters from you. Did you write? Nor have I had a letter from Captain Harris. There are many young fellows who would appreciate my attentions. One U.S. surveyor, David Walker, wants to court me. If Harris does not correspond, I may be obliged to entertain him.

I want you to be prepared for Mama and Papa's return. I fear for their safe travels, especially with the child. The other students enrolled in the Laredo School have younger parents than we do. In a few months, they have grown old and confused. They are bringing home our newest member of the family, a beautiful boy.

They need a lot of support for the baby. I am pleased both of you, and Nina, can make life easier for them.

I cannot describe the refinements I have learned here at the school. When I recall Rancho Refugio, I am embarrassed by how primitive our home life is. I believe our parents did their best, but I intend to do better when I establish my home, and someday, my family.

Until then, I wish you all the best and continue to remember you in my prayers.

Your Sister,
Dolores

Alicia and Clara sat in silence, considering the message, surrounded by the orderly house Maria had created. "Well, I guess we're ready for them to return."

"Is that all you have to say?" Clara said. "How dare she call us barbarians? What causes her to assume she can dump Captain Harris? Does she expect us to care for her child?"

"Dolores doesn't realize Harris has moved to the Philippines. She doesn't even know Nina is gone. I guess we could have written her at least once."

"Sure, she is sitting pretty in that fancy school. It's Mama and Papa we have to worry about, and the baby." Clara paced in the sala. "Here's what I think."

"I hope it doesn't include me doing childcare. Running the tie-up and doing official invoices for the clerk is all I can handle."

"You are spending too much time with that fellow, Valdez." The bickering began, like in the old days when they argued over silly things, those days before they realized how hard it was to run Rancho Refugio.

"You are right." Alicia put a quick end to the squabble. "Valdez brought me home late. That's all. I should have listened to you." She determined to leave out the details of her latest talk with Masagawa.

"You should always listen to me," Clara said.

"Tell me about your plan."

"While you've been running off with Valdez, I've been here watching Lupita care for her little brother. She helps her mother with all the chores and never loses track of the toddler or raises her voice, either. I can't imagine how she does it."

"I'll bet you imagine her caring for our new little brother. Is that it?"

"Were you thinking that too? We don't need any Native girls from the Mission to work for us when a good Mexican girl, the daughter of an officer, is right here."

Alicia winced to hear her sister's comment. A clanging noise, not too far from the patio, caught their attention.

"Aren't Valdez and the others gone yet?" Clara stepped to the gate and let out a cry.

"What is it?" Alicia walked to the door and saw three dark shadows running near the dock. Not compact figures like raccoons or foxes. They disappeared shortly after the girls spotted them. Three tall figures—it had to be men. The sisters bolted the door and peered out between the shutters.

After the initial clatter, all was quiet, but their nerves were on edge. They gathered up everything that could be used as a weapon, the fire irons, a hefty pot, a kitchen knife. Then they spent the night huddled before the fireplace, afraid to close their eyes. In the morning, they jumped when the door latch rattled.

"Alicia, it's me, Roberto. A ship anchored here," the young helper called. The girls shook themselves awake, tangled in their blankets and shawls. They tripped over the pots and fire irons before they opened the door just a crack.

"Did you have visitors earlier?" Roberto asked. "There are muddy tracks between the tie-up and the pathway to the cave. The anchor ropes are all jumbled up." Clara lunged out the front door.

"Let me look!" Deep ruts ran to the tie-up, as if something large had been dragged. Clara was halfway down the path when she spotted several men sauntering toward the house. "Halt right there. Who are you?"

39

Chapter

"Isn't this the famous Ortega dock? We thought you wanted trade," one man declared, as his mates snickered behind him. The sight of Clara, so distressed and disheveled, entertained them.

"Get back to your dinghy. Someone will be down to work. Unload your merchandise." Clara sounded fierce, but Alicia realized she was in a panic. Meanwhile, Alicia scrambled into her dungarees, boots and cap. Glad to see Roberto, she prayed his mother and siblings would be right behind him.

"Get the ledger and that fire iron, too," Alicia grabbed some lemons and oranges off the table. Fresh citrus always made the sailors more friendly.

"Welcome to the dock." Alicia tossed the oranges in the sailor's direction. Clara slunk back into the sala.

"Well, that was quite a welcome, nothing like what we expected." The sailors tossed the fruit between themselves.

"Roberto, tie up their lines. I'll require a signature for these goods. What was your last port?" Alicia did her best to sound abrupt and businesslike. The sooner she could send these fellows on their way, the better. Who had lurked around the property last night? She noticed the men's boots, all of them caked with mud. "You said your last port was Vanilla?" The grubby sailors doubled over with laughter.

"Not Vanilla, little missy, Manila. Don't you know? It's in the Philippines." The Philippines. That was all Alicia needed to hear. It was obvious who told these scoundrels to come to Rancho Refugio. Skipping the remaining paperwork, she closed the ledger on the troublemakers.

"You're finished here. Be on your way and Godspeed." The sailors pulled away from the hookup, waving their invoice, still laughing and repeating, "vanilla."

Private Valdez's wagon, filled with Roberto's family, pulled into the hacienda grounds. Clara and Alicia were relieved to see them.

"We need to talk." Clara startled Manuel with her serious expression. "Maria, we will be back soon." She tugged on Manuel's arm. "Come down to the cave, this way. I've got to make certain everything is secure."

"Clara, are you sure?" Alicia worried her sister would reveal the family secrets to Manuel.

"Ladies, what is going on? You seem so upset." Manuel inspected the grounds. He retraced the footsteps and ruts left near the pathway. Alicia imagined she saw footprints leading into the cave. The sisters gave Manuel the details of the night intruders and the men from Manila.

"You should both go to see the tax clerk with me today," he said.

"But why? We cannot leave the property unguarded after what happened last night."

"Alicia was going to see the clerk and learn about the proper forms. We can make the trip together. Señora Rodriguez and her children are here in the daylight," Manuel said.

"But, why?" Alicia wanted to go alone with Manuel. She wanted to keep the dock business, and Manuel, to herself.

"I suspect your dock has become too famous with the wrong people. I'm not suggesting you have anything to hide, but—" Manuel tried to finish.

"Hide? What makes you suspect we're hiding something? Who do you think you are talking to in this manner?" Clara took a quick look into the cave and saw that their treasure was still secure. Then she shooed Manuel away from the cave and back to the house.

"He's only trying to help us," said Alicia. "Let's listen."

"All I'm saying is, people talk. The buccaneers who use this anchor are the worst people. Let's go visit the pueblo authorities." Manuel reached out a hand to help the sisters onto his wagon. Soon, the sisters sat before the tax clerk.

"Why did your papa use this type of invoice, señorita Ortega?" The tax clerk was ready for the sisters' visit. He wore spectacles low on his nose and spoke to Alicia and Clara. The tiny office was crowded and stuffy.

"What do others use as dock records?" A stack of Alicia's recent invoices lay beside a gigantic government ledger on the desk. The clerk reached into a glass-front bookcase behind his chair and retrieved several dusty books.

"We have our pueblo accounts, like this. And the territorial records, like this one. There's the shipping ledger. And the overland trade journal, here. None of them are like what you brought me." Alicia imagined the official ledgers lecturing her, saying "Do this. It is the law, you stupid girl."

40

Chapter

lara gazed around the dusty corners of the clerk's tiny space while Alicia endured the humiliation of her ignorance. She regretted the day she'd copied Harris's phony documents to produce her invoices. Why did she follow the example of a cheat and a scoundrel? She realized the answer: because he was a man. She assumed he understood what he was doing.

"Papa can sometimes be old-fashioned." She made up a lie. "I'm sure it's time for us to adopt the example that you recommend for our dock records, señor." Alicia hated to disrespect Papa, but he was to blame for their situation.

"This is pretty." Feeling left out, Clara tried to insert herself in the conversation. She pointed to a fancy script page with an image of the Mexican flag in full color and traced her finger over the lettering.

"Ah, yes, it is very attractive, young lady." The clerk pulled the page from her reach and dusted it with his handkerchief. "I think our territorial shipping ledger is what you should use from now on." He presented a plain form at which Clara turned up her nose. "Allow me to provide you with some copies."

"My favorite Ortega sisters, how delightful to see you." From out of nowhere, Padre Romo leaned halfway into the tiny office. "Is your business about done here? I have someone else for you to meet."

"Padre?" How did he know they were in town? "We can't; we are doing work here." Clara was eager to get home.

Alicia picked up the new packet of forms and gathered her things to depart. As soon as she walked out of the office, Padre Romo moved close to her side.

"Alicia, tell me what happened last night." The padre spoke with urgency. He had heard about the intruders and knew there was gold stored somewhere at Rancho Refugio. "We must secure your shells." He introduced a stout fellow in a grey topcoat. "May I present our banker for all the town's valuables?" This was his attempt to safeguard the family fortune.

"Ladies, at your service. I've always admired your papa, but our paths never crossed," the banker said. "We treat all the affairs of our customers with the greatest discretion."

"Perhaps another time, señor." Clara stepped outside. Manuel waited near the bookkeeper's office. Romo boarded a wagon that waited behind Manuel's carriage. The banker boarded a third wagon behind that. "We must return, Private Valdez. I hope they are not planning to follow us." A parade of carriages headed to the rancho.

When the wagons arrived at the hacienda, the girls saw the front door standing wide open. Workers hauled enormous trunks into the residence. An old man and woman sat fanning their faces. Maria's children played in the yard, and Lupita stood in the shade caressing a little bundle.

"Stop here. What's going on?" Clara looked for signs of strangers or danger. Everyone was familiar. They acted content and happy. "Is this why they followed us? Some sort of surprise?"

"What do you know about this, Manuel?" Alicia said. Manuel did not respond.

"Your parents are home at last, ladies!" Padre Romo jumped from his seat and hurried toward the house.

This was not the homecoming Alicia imagined for her parents. She wished she'd paid more attention to Dolores's letter. After a day with the tax clerk, then delays by Padre Romo and the banker, this crowd surprised her. She realized, with a shock, the two old people on the veranda were Mama and Papa. "Clara, look."

"That's Mama and Papa. Lupita must be holding our baby brother," Clara said.

"Welcome home, Ortega, I have been longing to meet you." Even the banker approached Papa. They hugged like old friends, but Mama didn't stand up.

"Mama?" All the tension of the last months emptied in a rush of tears. Alicia embraced Mama. She felt her bony shoulders and frail body. Papa looked at his old-time friend, Padre Romo, with confusion in his face. Just how terrible a toll had the travel taken on her parents?

"Your family needs you now," said Maria Rodriguez. "I will gather my children. Private Valdez is ready to drive us." She made the sign of the cross on her forehead. "Thank God they made it home."

"Señora, will you allow Lupita to remain? She can be a great help here," Clara said. "Look how she already holds our baby brother."

"She would like to care for the child." Maria whispered to Lupita who rocked the infant in her arms and smiled at Clara and Alicia. His blanket fell aside from his face and he looked up with large blue eyes.

41
Chapter

"*ebidas!*" Papa called for brandy all around. Romo and the other men followed him into the sala.

"I recall I have a bottle hidden someplace." Papa's old bottle was not as full as he remembered. The shot glasses were in place and instantly five were filled to the brim. "*¡Salud!*" Papa led the initial toast.

Padre Romo and the banker offered their own toasts. One driver handed out cigars, and the men puffed clouds of smoke throughout the sala. Papa reached deeper into the cupboard and found a second bottle. He was worn out and disoriented after days of travel, but toasting and smoking in his own sala with men from the pueblo, Papa regained his spirit and vitality.

Mama's strength was ebbing. She stayed seated on the patio, where the afternoon air was cooling. Alicia could see she needed to rest.

"Girl, bring me the baby." Mama said, with her last bit of energy. The infant was already fast asleep in Lupita's arms. "This is your new brother, girls." Mama gave her daughters a faint smile.

"Yes, Mama, he is precious." Alicia resisted an urge to touch him. "And my goodness, his eyes." Clara managed a nod but said nothing.

"Papa was excited to bring him home." Mama struggled to her feet; Clara took her by the arm. "But your papa's youth is fading. He became confused more than once on the trip." Her tone was confidential. She glanced toward Lupita, who stayed apart. "Your papa called the baby by your name, Alicia, several times." Alicia blushed to imagine herself a child in her papa's mind. "I worry about how he will handle the dock. Have you told her, Clara?"

"Yes, Mama, I did as you asked, on her birthday."

"How will he manage our gold? We must help him," Mama said.

The girls did not want to trouble her with news of the intruders. Earlier that morning Padre Romo warned the sisters about thieves. Even the tax clerk urged them to move their money to the vaults in the pueblo.

"Oh Clara, I'm glad that Mama and Papa have finally returned, but how will he react to all we have done in his absence?" Alicia kept her voice low, worried that Mama would hear.

"The men will drink and talk it out. Papa will make the right decision," Clara said. "Mama, this girl's name is Lupita. She can stay here to support us with the child."

"Lupita, a lovely name, she looks like our Nina." Mama glanced at the young girl's face. "Take the baby now, please."

"What is his name?" Lupita uttered her first words in presence of the Ortegas. They all laughed at the question. "I like to call him Blue Eyes."

"Don't say that!" Alicia and Clara spoke at the same time. There was no mistaking Harris's ocean-blue eyes. How could they expect anyone to ignore them?

"In time, we will host a celebration and give this fine boy a formal name," Mama said. Manuel turned his wagon toward the pueblo. Maria's children were all snuggled in back. He offered a short wave and Alicia nodded to him as he drove away. Let us see what tomorrow brings, she thought.

42
Chapter

The noisy conversation in the sala, and the brandy-soaked toasts, continued into the wee hours of the morning.

"It was a boatload of sailors, returned from the Philippines, drunk, same as most men on shore leave." The banker tried to keep his voice low, but it echoed through the house.

Alicia shared a bed with Clara in the sleeping loft like they did when they were little girls. Mama, Lupita, and the baby slept in the rear bedroom. Clara snored, but Alicia heard the men downstairs sharing stories about the intruders.

"Everyone at the *cantina* overheard the sailors tell stories about 'the Ortega girls' and 'Refugio gold.' Who knows where they picked up that gossip?"

Alicia could not rest. She listened for any noises of intruders returning. She prayed the wagons and lights would warn them off. Still, she wished Roberto would stay to guard the cave and Manuel was there to keep watch.

"The Ortega name is famous. You should use a vault at the bank, nothing less." Padre Romo's liquor spoke.

"We have never used such a thing." Papa sounded annoyed, listening to these men discuss his private business.

"You never needed to protect so many children. Think about the girls and your new son. We are no longer young men, God help us."

"I am thinking of my children. I want you to bless my boy, here, at the hacienda, in a celebration for the whole pueblo." Alicia heard the pride in his voice. After many cups of brandy, his emotions were apparent. She felt a twinge of jealousy.

"I have never before placed conditions on my blessings, but this time, I must say no."

Alicia's heart paused. Did the padre refuse because the baby was the illegitimate child of Dolores and Harris?

"No?" Papa's voice boomed.

"What is it?" Clara awoke and rolled over.

"Just listen," Alicia said.

"I will bless the boy when his inheritance is safe in the pueblo's bank. That is my condition. Of course, I must be the *padrino*!" The men cheered Romo's declaration.

"Nonsense!" Papa leaned toward Romo and said, "It will take forever to clear out the cave." That's why Romo panicked when he heard about intruders on the property.

"You have trustworthy friends here tonight. We have two wagons, five healthy men, and the cover of darkness. Let's take action. Then we can celebrate your new heir." Romo must have been preparing for this all along.

Once Mama and Papa got settled back into their hacienda routine, they planned the baby's naming ceremony. After a month of preparation, the house was elaborately decorated and the entire pueblo was invited. Papa squeezed into his old military jacket for the special occasion of his son's formal blessing.

"Just because you can still button that old jacket across your belly, do not expect me to salute." Mama studied her chubby husband and remembered the day when they first met at the Presidio.

"You are as lovely as the day we met." Papa's compliment made her remember and blush. She could not help thinking of those memories of her life as a young lady at the Presidio.

She recalled the days when she and her cousin, Marie Theresa, were thrilled to meet the soldiers and the brave men in the Portolá expedition. The two young ladies were so admired. They were among the few young Mexican women within hundreds of miles. The hostess of the gala event was *la señora de la Guerra*, whose husband served as the *comandante* of the Presidio. Then, she noticed her reflection in the mirror. "Just look at my face now, so dry and freckled. My hands are blistered after years of planting gardens around this hacienda." She lost her youth plucking chickens and knotting fishing nets to feed her family. She served Papa's brothers before they married neophyte Chumash girls who delivered sons, when all she could produce were three daughters after twenty years of marriage. Then she remembered the celebration of the day.

"Now, we have a son to celebrate as our heir."

43

Chapter

"Blessings on you all." The crowd overflowed downstairs from the sala, onto the patio, and scattered on the garden paths. "Gather around here." Romo tried to call everyone to order.

Mama sat with the celebrated boy on her lap. Papa stood behind her, puffing out his chest and holding in his stomach in his uniform. The girls stood on either side of their papa. Both girls looked grown up in their mother's old gowns.

"You've gained a son, but you seem to have lost a daughter, señor Ortega." There was an awkward moment when Dolores's absence was noted.

"Oh yes," Papa said. "She studies in Laredo. We are all proud of her." The crowd nodded and murmured.

"The family is a precious gift and we are here to bless the youngest heir to the Ortega legacy, Carlos Antonio Ortega." Everyone gathered responded with cheers, and the ladies genuflected their blessings. Alicia and Clara were pushed aside as the guests rushed forward around Mama and young Carlos. The sisters noticed some women get one peek at Carlos's blue eyes and whisper behind their fans. The girls could not help but overhear their papa's conversation.

"You are right. A man's daughters will marry and leave home, but a boy will inherit the land and carry on his name." He lifted his glass. "To my son!"

"A son!" The room erupted in a spontaneous toast.

"This is the reason we are here today to celebrate," Padre Romo said. "There is no substitute for a son."

"Are we done here?" Alicia did not join in the toast. Her brother took all the time and energy of the household. To hear Papa brag about him and expect her to disappear infuriated her. She excused herself to the patio. Mama handed the baby to the nursemaid and followed.

"How far away are Laredo and Monterey? How soon can I get there?" Alicia glanced at her Mama, then looked up at the night sky, recalling Manuel's description of the stars in Orion's belt.

"What are you saying? You'll always be here with us." Mama brushed her skirts and nodded to guests passing by. "Carlos will need a teacher. You remember when your big sister, Dolores, taught you?"

"He won't need a tutor. Everyone says he's the smartest boy they've ever seen." She imitated the pompous tone Papa used when he spoke about his son. She could not bear to think of being his tutor. Ever since her bleeding began, angry feelings crept up in her. Once, she loved the rancho. Lately she dreamed of travel and a new life far away.

"We are a family, mija. You and your sisters are as important as baby Carlos." Alicia could not believe her.

"Dolores is away, and she is a part of the family. Clara and I kept the rancho for a year. We are grown and you have a new child to enjoy."

"Yes, a baby, and your papa, and the rancho. It takes all of us working together." Mama kept nodding to guests, accepting the gifts they brought Carlos. "Thank you; you are too kind."

"Did you know, even Nina is having a child? She moved to Monterey. We are all grown up." She remembered the sad day of Nina's departure.

"Is that where she has been? Would you like to visit Nina?" Alicia was so surprised by Mama's suggestion she wanted to hold her to it.

"Can we write to Tío Salvador in the morning? He invited us to Monterey when he was here inspecting the dock taxes."

"Your tío was here? No one has told us this!" Mama's full attention turned to her daughter. "Taxes? What taxes did he inspect? Who else knows this?" She looked into the house to find her husband and pulled Alicia toward the sala.

"Everyone knows," she said. "He left something for Papa and I forgot about it."

"What did he leave? You go find it right now and bring it here." Mama's temper was building even as she tried to greet lingering guests. "And find your sister, Clara, too."

Alicia climbed to the sleeping loft where she found Clara sulking by herself. She had already changed out of Mama's gown into her own party dress. She stared out the window, not wanting to rejoin the party.

"We had more fun when it was just you and me," Clara said. "I cannot sleep through the night with that baby crying."

"What are you doing up here? We've got to find that big envelope Tío Salvador left. They don't know about everything that we went through while they were in Laredo. All they care about is baby Carlos."

The official envelope was buried beneath the sleeping crates and a pile of blankets. Still smooth and sealed, it had not been touched since Tío left it; Alicia had never dared to look inside.

The party celebrated Carlos Antonio, but much more news was about to be shared.

44

Chapter

apa took control once the guests were gone. Only Padre Romo remained with the family members. Alicia held on to the documents from Tío Salvador.

"Give me that envelope. Tell me exactly what happened here when I was away," Papa said.

"Come sit, ladies." Padre Romo waved Mama, Clara, and Alicia to the table, then poured Papa another brandy. Baby Carlos squirmed on Mama's lap.

"This is my home, built with my two hands, my own sweat and blood." Papa began his tirade. "Nothing happens here without my consent. I demand to know what happened while your Mama and I were assisting your sister in Laredo." He tossed down a swallow of brandy. "The Ortega men run this rancho, and not any woman. Do you understand?"

Clara crossed her arms over her chest and scowled at Papa. Mama shook her head and raised her eyes toward her altar. It was Alicia who scooted back her chair, wanting to leave the table.

"No, please, sit. If I may, Ortega?" Papa nodded to the padre, who crossed himself. "This is a night for rejoicing. Let us continue in that spirit. I, for one, am thankful for each Ortega at this table, men and women."

"Don't think that you will ever replace me, Padre," Papa said. Romo looked Papa square in the face.

"God gave me the privilege to be a part of this family. Since the night of the shipwreck, and all that happened afterward, even over this last year."

"You may know our family history, but I am still the head of this house."

"Papa! Forgive him, Padre, he did not mean to be disrespectful," Mama said.

"Hush, woman. I want to know what went on behind my back when I was in Laredo."

"Papa, did you notice how organized the dock looked when you returned?" Clara leaned across the table toward Papa. Her fists clenched. "Captain Harris cleaned up your mess. See the repairs on the house, the patio and in the garden? That was done by Maria Rodriguez and her family. The padre sent her to help us."

"And where is Harris, anyway?" Papa glanced around the sala, noticing how nice everything looked.

"Maria's son, Roberto, helps sell items from the dock and her daughter, Lupita, is taking care of your son Carlos." Clara had never stood up to Papa before, nor defended anyone but herself. "That happened behind your precious back!" She fell back in her chair, exhausted.

"What is this paper you have given me?" Papa tore open the envelope, ignoring Clara and the seal of the governor. "This is Salvador Tenorio's name signed here. What is he doing in my business? He has always wanted to take our land, the greedy Spaniard."

"He was a perfect gentleman," Padre Romo said.

"Ha, he's a pirate and has no business on my rancho," Papa said. He let the papers drop onto the edge of the table.

"Papa, Tío Salvador works for the governor. Look at his seal on this envelope." Alicia snatched up the papers. "Tío tried to help us. Your taxes were never paid, and he was sent here to inspect."

"We don't need his help. I did not ask him to come here."

"Something else happened when you were gone. Alicia had her fifteenth birthday, and I told her everything about the Ortega fortune in the cave," Clara said.

"So that's why that banker was after my treasure!" Papa said. "You girls have been talking outside the family about our fortune."

"Calm yourself, Ortega. Your brave girls took action to pay your taxes. One more day and you would have lost the land grant. I helped them a little," Padre Romo said.

"You? You touched my treasure?" Papa said.

"The girls brought it to me. One day before Salvador Tenorio had to make his report. Only one week before men came at night to steal from your secret cave. That is why I brought the banker to help you set up an official account the very day you returned to Rancho Refugio. This is true, so help me God." Padre Romo said.

When the anger and excitement around the table ran its course, Mama and Papa stared at their girls in disbelief. Clara and Alicia leaned against one another, having spent themselves in revealing their fearful actions. Padre Romo stood.

"What does this document from the governor have to say?" The padre turned toward Alicia, who held the papers up and read.

"This docking station, Rancho Refugio, forty leagues north of the Mexican port in Santa

Barbara, Alta California, on the Arturo Ortega land granted by the President of the Mexican Republic, shall serve as an Official Substation and a Shallow Water Refuge for all vessels domestic and foreign under the following rights and restrictions: docking personnel and help from the local Presidio, protection and defense by the national forces and regular inspections and taxation by territorial authorities."

By Order of Gov. Fagas,
Alta California, 24 de Julio, 1830.

"Papa, we are official, no longer a black-market port for buccaneers and thieves like—" Alicia stopped herself from saying the rest. After all that they had been through with the gold, the taxes, Captain Harris, and even Nina leaving with the trapper, what else could go wrong?

45

Chapter

"What did that Spanish pirate, Tenorio, have to do with this?" Papa suspected anything to do with Tío Salvador. "Will he bother me about taxes from now on?"

"Your account in the territorial bank will cover all of that." Padre Romo poked his finger toward baby Carlos's tummy. "The land is secure for the life of this little one. Also, any heirs that come after him, praise the good Lord."

"Alicia, you were right, we should write to Tío Salvador." Mama's apology was sincere. "It seems we have a lot to thank him for."

There was nothing left to say. Even baby Carlos slept through that night. Papa slept in his favorite chair after reminiscing with Padre Romo, who stretched out on the couch. Alicia and Clara retired to the sleeping loft swearing they would never grow old, or doubt their children, or lose their temper, especially not in front of the padre. The rancho seemed secure, and the family was together. Another boat was approaching the dock.

Chickens squawked in the yard early the next morning. Roberto passed among them, collecting eggs. His mama Maria and Chata, his sister, dragged gunny sacks through the yard and gardens collecting trash from the party the night before. Lupita was the first one to leave the house with baby Carlos on her hip. He was ready to eat the moment he awoke.

"Is Private Valdez here? I have some family news that may help him." Alicia watched Lupita speak to Maria from the window in the sleeping loft. Could she be trusted with all she'd heard last night?

"Good morning to little Carlos." Manuel Valdez approached the women. Lupita filled him in on all the family news of the previous night. He used the early hours to inspect the dock and hoped to linger until he saw Alicia. She spotted him from the window and rushed to dress.

It was the day after the big party. Mama and Papa came to grips with all that had happened in their absence. Alicia did not want to give up her role on the dock. Roberto assumed Papa would be his new boss now.

"Any ships expected today? Where is your papa? Does he need my help?" Roberto said.

"I want your help. He's sleeping off the party." Alicia announced her agenda. "We need a new dock sign. We are now official!"

"I can make a sign. What do you mean, official?" Roberto walked around the property to find scraps of wood for a new sign.

"Was this your Tío Salvador's doing?" Manuel caught up with Alicia. He looked as if he had something more important to say to her, but instead he busied himself watching Roberto rummaging for wood. "An influential man, your Tío."

"Find a place for this sign." Alicia wanted to tell Manuel about her plan to write to Tío Salvador and visit Monterey, but something held her back. He was not really a member of the family. He was just a soldier, someone who helped Maria and her family because of his Presidio job.

Roberto collected wood scraps, a pole, and some charcoal for a sign for the dock. They rigged a placard together. "*Puerto Oficial*" it read. They put the Mexican flag above it and stood back to inspect their work.

"What is this?" Papa approached. "And who are you two young men?" Alicia's back stiffened when she heard his voice. Roberto and Manuel stopped their work and turned to face Papa.

46

Chapter

"Good morning." Alicia watched Papa approach, still pulling up his suspenders. "Maria's son, Roberto, is here to help us."

"Help?" Papa inspected the fresh sign and flag. "Your mama and the other women need you at the house. Go now." He dismissed her without saying a word to Roberto, who watched her go.

Maria and Lupita continued cleaning up the mess the partygoers left behind. Mama and Clara slept late. What did Papa expect Alicia to do at the house? She straightened the table, propped up the governor's proclamation, then laid her hand on Harris's ledger book. Look at this ridiculous thing, she thought.

Alicia took out her anger toward Papa on the phony ledger. She ripped it apart and used the pieces to frame the statement from the governor. An hour later, when Mama appeared for her coffee, she was writing a message to Tío Salvador.

"Listen to this, Mama: To our dear Tío Salvador Tenorio, our family appreciates the many gifts and favors you have granted us."

"Scratch that out." Mama looked over her shoulder at the note. "A government man receiving those lines from his family would be suspected of favoritism. You don't want to get him in trouble, do you?" The day had barely begun and already Alicia was directed by both her parents.

"Write this," Mama continued. " 'To the Honorable Salvador Tenorio, Assistant to the Territorial Governor of Alta California, Secretary of Coastal Waterways, Permits & Taxes.' No, no. That is all part of his title." Alicia listened, amazed with her Mama's vocabulary and talent.

"Who is talking down there?" Clara joined the conversation. "Mama?"

"Hush, mija. Write this: 'We send you commendations, giving notice to the governor of your expertise and excellent performance of your territorial duties carried out here at Rancho Refugio, Alta California. We, our properties, and our loyalties are ever after at your service.'"

"That's a very long sentence, Mama." Alicia dipped her pen in ink to finish the line.

"That's the way they like it." Mama brushed back her graying hair. She had a small smile on her lips, caught up in a memory of her past life.

"How do you know all this? I've never seen you write a letter before." Clara rummaged around for a clean cup for her coffee. "It's all gone!"

"Girls who sleep too late miss the morning coffee." Mama returned to the letter.

"Remember, I used to read the letters coming to the comandante. I worked for his wife at the Presidio." Alicia tried to imagine her Mama before she was a wife and mother. "Those altered gowns you wore last night were from my days in the society of officers and government officials. You could have been the daughters of . . ." She didn't finish her sentence but took her cup outside.

"Why did she marry our papa?" Clara blurted out.

"Her letter is definitely better than mine." Alicia was thinking the same thing about Papa. "But it is missing the most important part. Let's add it here."

"What? Let me see." Clara leaned in to look at the letter. Alicia added:

> Thank you for your invitation to Monterey.
> Our two daughters would be pleased to make
> the journey.
> We appreciate your kind hospitality.
> Señor A. Ortega,
> Rancho Refugio, Alta California.

"Really? Can we go to Monterey? You and I? Tío Salvador asked me if I wanted to visit Monterey and I do, I do!" Clara danced around the sala.

"We can ask. He invited both of us." Alicia kept a wary eye on her mama. "He has been very good to us."

"Can you imagine going all that way?"

"Look at this document. I've been studying it this morning." She lifted the newly framed declaration and pointed to a line near the bottom. "It says 'help from the local Presidio, protection and defense by the national forces.' I think we deserve some of that help."

47

Chapter

The sisters were so busy and excited about their proposed journey they noticed nothing else happening around the property, the garden, or out at the tie-up. It was nearly time for the noon meal. Maria and Lupita prepared to serve the family.

"Where is your papa?" Mama entered, carrying little Carlos and clutching a bunch of flowers for the table. "He needs to come and wash for lunch." She laid the baby on the rug. Carlos could now roll over and scoot around on his belly. "Go call him. Clara, you help me here with these flowers."

Alicia started down to the dock where a dingy loaded with cargo floated on the water. No shipping traffic was anticipated, but here was a new trader. Papa and another man stood talking while Roberto pulled boxes out of the dinghy. As she got close, Alicia could hear Papa's usual bragging and exaggeration.

"The biggest, the best, the smartest." Papa's hands flew up and down emphasizing his tall tales. He was obviously talking about baby Carlos. The scruffy sailor wore a hood over his head and kept nodding as Papa talked.

"What have you got in these boxes? They are not very heavy." Roberto was trying to keep track of the cargo. Alicia was glad Roberto did such a good job, especially since Papa was distracted by his conversation and ignored the off-loaded goods. There was something familiar about the way this other fellow in the hood stood on the dock.

"Official, eh? That's new." The trader raised his head and nodded toward the new government sign. "Those are fine silk kimonos, young man. My wife and her relatives make them. Take care."

Alicia caught the tone of his voice and the sun caught the glint in Captain Harris's blue eyes. She hoped and prayed she was mistaken.

"Lunch, Papa." Alicia kept her distance. She was not prepared to see Harris and knew it would devastate Clara to see him after all this time. She had heard the trader say, "My wife."

"You must join us." Papa kept talking, unaware that this man he spoke to was the one person the Ortega family wanted to forget.

"Roberto, stay with this fellow and finish his business." Alicia made her way back to the house as fast as she could. "Follow me, Papa."

Alicia called out as she rushed into the sala, "Lupita!" She was out of breath and had to work fast. Did Papa follow her? "Take Carlos to the back room."

"Your Papa always likes to see *Carlitos* at lunch. The baby can stay."

"He'll get cranky, Mama." Alicia resisted giving the boy a slight pinch to help prove her point. Hearing his name, Carlos fussed anyway, and Lupita picked him up and carried him off.

"Clara?" She put a hand on her sister's shoulder.

"Do you want me to go, too? What's gotten into you?" Clara was already snacking on fried potatoes.

"Just be calm, sister. That is all I ask." There was no time to explain. Papa entered, and the man from the dock entered behind him. Clara drew in a sharp breath and clutched her hands over her mouth. Mama looked bewildered. Maria handed Papa and the stranger damp towels to clean their hands and faces. Then it was Mama's turn to gasp.

"Harris?"

"What Harris? This man sailed in from the Philippines. His wife makes silk kimonos. He brought boxes of them," Papa said. "Where is baby Carlos? I've been telling him all about our boy."

"His wife?" Clara stared up at Harris.

"Look, his eyes are like the baby's." As soon as Papa said this, he recognized Harris. His gaze darted around the room, looking for the baby.

"He's asleep, Papa." Alicia turned toward Harris. "I do not believe you have a permit to trade here, sir." She could not believe her own boldness. "You have worn out your welcome."

"But, but," Harris sputtered in protest. "Alicia, Clara, you have grown up."

"Such a long time with no word from you." Clara found her voice.

"You missed your chance with my daughters, sir." Papa came to his senses and his courage. "Your goods are not welcome here."

Everyone could hear baby Carlos howling from the back of the residence. The infant cried whenever he was separated from the rest of the family.

"Let me look at this boy. He sounds just like one of my own sons," Harris said.

"One of your sons?" Clara thumped her forehead on the table. Mama stood as Harris took a step toward the cry of his child.

"Carlos is our son." Papa grabbed Harris by the arm and dragged him to the door. "Our son, Carlos Antonio Ortega, has the boldest cry of all babies in creation. He will make a fine heir to Rancho Refugio. Adiós, señor Harris."

If he tried to stay, Harris knew the four women and one old man would protect the child to their last breath. Finally, defeated and dejected, Harris retrieved his merchandise and disappeared forever.

The best and the worst all happened in one brief visit. Alicia's wish to have Harris banished from the rancho was granted. Clara's heartbreak, and Mama and Papa's lie about their son, were laid bare. It was a quiet lunch. Only baby Carlos, resting in Mama's arms, gurgled and cooed, a reminder of the day's events.

Days passed, and Clara would not leave the sleeping loft. Alicia visited her with special teas and quiet words. Mama and Papa did not know why Clara was so upset. They carried on as if nothing unusual had happened, covering the footprints of their own dishonesty.

Maria kept the house in order, Lupita minded the baby, and Roberto minded the dock. On the third day after Harris departed, Private Manuel Valdez visited the hacienda in full dress uniform. He carried a message for Papa.

"Who is this soldier boy?" Papa did not recognize Valdez, but seeing him in uniform reminded him of his own youthful days in military service. Days when hope lay ahead of him.

"A letter, sir, from the comandante." Manuel made a little bow. His eyes searched the sala for Alicia, whom he had missed seeing in the last few days.

48

Chapter

"This looks official. Clara, we have a letter."
Papa thought he understood women's moods
after all the years with his wife and daughters. He called Clara, hoping to cheer her up.

"From Dolores?" Clara could not suppress her curiosity.

"From the comandante himself. You are the oldest child
here; you read it."

"As you wish, Papa." Clara glanced around the sala at her
family. Then her gaze lingered on Manuel Valdez. She drew
herself up with a serious expression and read, "To the Honorable
A. Ortega."

"Read that again." Papa enjoyed being addressed as honorable. Clara continued to read. "This voucher, under the Docking
Substation Declaration of July 24, 1820, provides for docking
personnel, protection, and defense from the local Presidio and
begins the employ of the following persons for service."

"What? Who?" Papa tried to snatch the papers but Clara read on.

"Workers for the dock and our escort for travel to Monterey," Alicia said.

"What travel?"

"Didn't I mention, there is an invitation for our girls to visit their Tío Salvador in Monterey? Such a gracious man, we owe him this courtesy, don't you think?"

"Did you say, two men for the dock?" Papa waved off Mama's comments and turned to his own interests. "One boy has been sufficient for the dock, and he works for free." Now he took the letter from Clara's hands. "I guess if the comandante wants to spend this money we will take it. I know the man I will choose."

"Papa, we can pay Roberto." Alicia said. "Who do you have in mind?"

"A man who belongs here, old Ernesto. He washed up on this shore so long ago."

"The drunkard?" Clara said.

"He has known more sorrow than your silly romances will ever cause, young lady. He will join us here and you will give him respect."

"And the escort, for our daughter's visit to show our thanks to Tío Salvador?" Mama stood next to Private Valdez. He looked the part of an official Presidio escort.

"Women. Beware of the females in your life, my young private. You will learn they are always making plans. Come with me, Alicia, we will go give Roberto this news."

"Should we take Maria, his mama?" Alicia was not sure Papa remembered that Roberto was Maria's son.

"No. A boy likes to tell his mama about his first job by himself." Alicia tried to imagine Papa telling his mama about his first job.

They walked toward the dock; the flag waved over the co-mandante's proclamation. Roberto maintained everything, but he was nowhere in sight. As they waited for him to return, Papa reminisced.

"I'm sorry I was not here for your quinceañera, your fif-teenth birthday, Alicia. It has special meaning for the Ortega girls. Your mama and I decided, years ago, that we would gift our children the story of our blessings, our treasure, on their fifteenth birthdays."

"Clara told me, Papa. But I still have questions. I would rather hear the story from you."

"Our stories change as we grow older and wiser." Papa pulled his jacket around him. The dock grew cooler. "What you and Clara, and your Tío Salvador, have done will change our story forever."

"We paid the taxes, nothing more."

"You removed the shame from our family name and made this an official port. I did what I thought was right the night of the shipwreck, but I am not proud of it. There were many drowning men and too few of us to save them all. There were chests of gold at our feet and we were unpaid scouts, hungry and hopeless. God forgive us." He looked at the Pacific, as if he could hear the sailors calling out for help. A pained expression hung on his face.

Alicia realized these were the most honest words and emo-tions she had ever heard from her papa. Father and daughter, he confided in her as if she were an old trusted friend.

"Some suspected us over the years. The secret lived with me and my brothers until we fought so much, they left me here on the rancho with its dark memories." Papa shaded his eyes from the sun glaring on the water. "Oh, what I would give to see them again."

"That is all past now, Papa. Let your memories heal." Alicia touched the sign, "Puerto Oficial," and considered what it cost her Papa. "We have the future, Carlos's future, to look forward to."

"What will Carlos's future be, I wonder? I saw how quickly things were changing in Laredo. There were many Americans. Scouts, trappers, and surveyors; men with greedy expressions working for the United States government. One of them, a man named David Walker, has his eye on your sister Dolores." Alicia could not help but flinch when she heard the word, "trapper."

"Soon we will see them here. I wonder what future Carlos will have?" The thoughts her papa shared remained in Alicia's mind for a long time.

49

Chapter

"What shall we take? I need something new." Over the next month, Clara stayed busy with plans for the trip to Monterey. She spoke day and night about traveling clothes, dinner dresses, touring outfits and shoes, hats and scarfs to match it all.

The only thing on Alicia's mind was finding Nina in Monterey. She wondered if Nina's baby had come and hoped she would find them both in good health. So many children and mothers died during birthing. She worried about Nina's fate.

Clara assembled a pile of clothes in the loft. Alicia set aside one blank notebook and a favorite satchel.

"There is a fellow in the garden." Maria came in from the cooking ramada to report a stranger on the property.

"What does he look like?" Clara put down her packing.

"He looks woolly, with whiskers and long hair. He is humming to himself. Maybe he's loco." Maria led the sisters to the rear of the house to peek out in the backyard. Old Ernesto leaned against the shed where Papa lived with his brothers years ago. He looked woolly, his tattered pants and faded jacket blended in with the cabin that was only fit for firewood.

"We recognize him. It's old Ernesto." Alicia didn't tell Maria that Papa intended to have this man work with her son. "I'll go find Papa and let him know."

"Don't go out there alone, Maria. Wait till Papa comes." Clara remembered the time Ernesto arrived with Tío Salvador, singing like a crazy fellow.

"Ah, you remember the old shack, eh, Ernesto? It is good of you to come and help me make repairs." Papa was quick to greet his old friend like an honored guest, even though he looked like an aged tramp. The women watched from the back door, all three thinking neither the old drunk nor the cabin were fit for repair. "We all get old and require some fixing. Come down to the dock with me; we'll talk." Papa lead the man away.

"What's going on here?" Mama came to the doorway where the women shook their heads with disapproval. "Oh, is that Ernesto with your Papa? He was once such a handsome man."

"Oh, Mama, that cannot be true!" Clara said. "I hope Papa does not intend to let him in the house."

"He wants to clean the old cabin so Ernesto will have a place to sleep and work." Mama said. Lupita stood behind her holding baby Carlos. Mama held out a little piece of fruit for Carlos who stuffed it in his tiny mouth.

"You girls should be packing. Leave your Papa to his own business." The conversation shifted again to bonnets and blankets and tomorrow's journey.

Alicia watched. Papa did not go to the dock but toward the cave. He and Ernesto were not seen again for hours.

"I think I'll go check on Papa. It's almost time for the noon meal." Alicia could not control her curiosity. She slipped out, unnoticed by the other ladies.

Leaving the house, she could see Roberto all alone on the dock, so she went straight toward the cave that once guarded the family secrets. Then she saw her Papa, sitting on his jacket on the sand, watching Ernesto, who was halfway down the beach.

"Papa, what is he doing?" Alicia asked. "Should he be here with us and the baby?"

"He is family, Alicia. This is where we saved him from the sea. It's the place he remembers hearing the cries of his shipmates. I believe he is thinking of them now."

A large stone stood around 10 feet away from Papa. It had a white cross smeared on its surface. A line of stones trailed along the beach toward Ernesto, who knelt beside a bucket of whitewash with a stick in his hand. Beyond him an old shell mound, revered by Nina's people, rose from the sand. Something moved beside it.

"Is there someone beside Ernesto out there, Papa?" Alicia strained to see the shadowy figure. A faint puff of smoke hung in the air and shaded the figure.

"It may be Nina's grandma. I saw her here last week." Papa had never mentioned her before. Alicia was surprised that he knew anything about her.

"Grandma Masagawa? What's she doing?" Alicia started to walk toward her.

"No, wait. Wait until Ernesto is finished." Papa reached out to hold Alicia by the hand. "They are doing the same thing, remembering."

Alicia knew their lunch was ready, but some things were more important than lunch, or packing, or thinking only of tomorrow. Eventually, Ernesto placed his last rock in the sand and returned to Papa. The two men headed toward the house.

50

Chapter

Alicia walked toward the figure standing by the shell mound. It was Masagawa. She fanned her sage vapors north, south, east, and west and hummed a traditional chant. She did not look at Alicia but talked to her.

"You take greetings north and see Nina's new baba. Many moons wait for you." Alicia knew Masagawa was speaking of her long journey to Monterey.

"You still visit the mounds?" How did she manage to travel all this way from her new village? "You can come with me to see Nina."

"Masagawa live here now, with ancestors." She set down her abalone bowl of smoldering sage. Her wrinkled face and hands were browned from years of sun. "And the baba?"

"Little Carlos? You were right. His arrival put an end to Captain Harris at Rancho Refugio. You remembered my worries."

"Worries and blessings travel together in the same bundle. Mama and Papa understand this." Masagawa looked toward Papa and Ernesto walking away. Alicia wondered how much she knew about the shipwreck. It was not only the past that Alicia wondered about, but the future. What would become of Rancho Refugio and the village?

Back in the hacienda, Mama had given up on lunch by the time Alicia returned.

"We covered the bread and fruit for an early dinner. Just see who joined us." Padre Romo arrived to say farewell to Clara and Alicia. Private Valdez had his wagon ready to begin the journey in the morning. A black trunk, with room for Clara's wardrobe, was lashed to the wagon.

Valdez stood at attention in black shiny boots. He shifted his weight from side to side, nervous about his new assignment as an official escort. A small bundle Masagawa had given him for Alicia lay below his seat. Two horses were harnessed for the first day of the journey. Two more were tethered behind the wagon. The driver, assigned from the Presidio, was due to arrive at dawn.

"Now if your Papa would show his face, we could have our last meal together."

"No, not the last meal, Mama. Don't say that," Clara said. "It will be bad luck for our trip."

"I am here to guard against bad luck. Plus, I brought this special candle to bless Dolores in Laredo while we are all together today." They all watched Padre Romo place the candle in the middle of the table and light the flame. Alicia noticed how he waved his open palm over the flame. North, south, east, and west, as Masagawa did with her sage.

"Ooooh!" Baby Carlos watched the flame glow. Everyone laughed at his enthusiasm and Mama gave him a big kiss on the top of his head.

"That is the sound Dolores made as a child when we lit our candles!" Mama's eyes glistened with tears.

"Oh Mama, we miss her, too. Thank you for the blessing, Padre Romo." Alicia felt her own tears. "We can't leave out Mother Mary." Alicia reached out to Mama's altar to light Mother Mary's candle one last time.

"What have you got to pray about? All the horrible days have passed, and now we're going on a new journey," Clara said.

"I envied Dolores when she left on her journey. I never imagined all the things that would happen here at home." Alicia's hand brushed over Nina's favorite manzanita broom below the altar. "Mama, will you light this candle for us while we are gone?"

"We will all pray for you," the padre said. "When you see Nina, give her my condolences on her grandma's death. I must admit, her remedies often helped ease the pain of my parishioners." Alicia thought she must have misunderstood him. There was no time to ask because Papa arrived, drawing everyone's attention.

"And who will miss me, your dear papa? We can postpone this trip, you know." Papa broke the spell that the candle cast on everyone.

"Don't be silly, Papa." Clara frowned at Papa, surprised to see a tall man standing behind him. "Are you our driver?"

"No, ma'am," the stranger said. He was clean-shaven with a smudge of whitewash on his cuff. He nodded to Padre Romo.

"I believe this is our old friend señor Ernesto Seca, old Ernesto. Meet the Ortega daughters, and their new baby brother, Carlos Antonio Ortega."

"Ernesto will teach Roberto all he knows about ropes, ships, charts and all things nautical. He will teach our son when he has his sea legs."

Everyone laughed except Alicia. She pulled the padre to the side of the room.

"Is something wrong, Alicia?" Padre Romo said.

"I talked to her today. Masagawa." Alicia said. The padre crossed himself.

"Let us keep that to ourselves and count it as an extra blessing on your trip north and for the days come."

Coming Next:
Broken Promises

By Anita Perez Ferguson
Young Adult—Historical Fiction—Adventure

Josefina Duran Tenorio, sixteen, enjoyed the most adventurous treasure hunts with her friend Sola along the busy waterfront of Monterey in 1835. Mexico had just opened up the docks to international trade, and Monterey was California's sole port of entry, with shiploads of exotic cargo coming in daily from England, the Caribbean, and the United States.

Josephina's papa, Salvador, knew when every ship was due as a part of his job. The docks could be a perilous place for young girls to play. Josephina and Sola boldly traded with the sailors, bargained for trinkets, and sometimes mistreated their young tagalong friend, Sparrow, who was only twelve.

The docks attracted Americans—called "Yanquis"—to Monterey, some corrupt and dangerous. Many of them married into Mexican families and became Mexican citizens. Later, the Mexican rulers redistributed much of the local land formerly run by the Catholic Church and huge cattle ranches were formed. One of those ranches belonged to Josephina's family. But things were about to change.

The girls used Sparrow as their treasure-hunting spy, since no one noticed the tiny Native girl among the big ships and cargo boxes. She had a good memory for every story and rumor she overheard. One day she heard too much, and the fun of the treasure hunts became dangerous business for the girls and their families.

A US government agent named Larkin arrived in Monterey, announcing he was the first American Consulate in California. Sparrow overheard his secret plan to make the Mexican territory a part of the United States. The girls were afraid to tell the truth about Larkin. Who would believe them? And they were afraid about what it would mean to have their country taken away.

Thanks and Acknowledgments

Writing a story is, more or less, a solo act. The writer calls on her experience, imagination, and education. Her relationships can influence her thinking, but mainly, she is alone.

Publishing a book is a different exercise, one that requires the support and expertise of various people. I was fortunate to have many individuals and organizations assist me. I give them all my deep thanks.

My first thanks go to my newest partners, the crew at Bublish.com and especially Shilah LaCoe. Thanks to the person who introduced me to Bublish and other helpful resources, Alexa Bigwarfe at Women in Publishing. Thanks to my friends and colleagues at the Society for Children's Book Writers and Illustrators. Many thanks for the hospitality and education programs at the Old Mission Santa Barbara, the Santa Barbara Museum of Natural History, and the Santa Barbara Historical Museum. Special thanks go to a courageous group of beta readers who faithfully shared their responses to my early draft of this book. My dear friends from my NaNoWriMo writing group gave me daily motivation to go on with the publishing process, and finally, to my other friends and family for their endless patience and support. Thank you. Mil gracias.

Reference and Vocabulary Study Guide

I.   Captain Harris was a sailor from Boston.

See the real story of the man who sailed from Boston to Refugio, converted to Catholicism, and married the daughter of a land grant family.

https://goletahistory.com/the-man-who-named-goleta/

II.   Alicia and her sisters had no right to inherit their Papa's land grant.

The American colonies generally followed the same laws of their mother countries, usually England, France, or Spain. According to British law, the husband controlled a woman's property. Some colonies or states, however, gradually gave women limited property rights. See the history of Land Inheritance Laws for Females in the US.

https://www.thoughtco.com/property-rights-of-women-3529578

III. Nina's grandmother, Masagawa, used sage as a medicinal herb.

In Native American mythology, sage is one of the most important ceremonial plants, used by many tribes as an incense and purifying herb. Sweetgrass symbolizes protection and healing in many Native cultures and is considered to drive out evil influences and ward off bad luck. See Native American Indian sage medicine, meaning and symbols:

www.native-languages.org/legends-sage.htm

IV. Hide and tallow trade in early California

When the hides were burned at the Mission it had a terrible impact. The hide and tallow trade was big business at the missions in early California.

https://www.missionsjc.com/wp-content/uploads/MSJC_HIde_Tallow.pdf

V. Nina helped the trapper discover the trails around Refugio.

See the history of surveyors and trappers in California in the 1800s.

https://en.wikipedia.org/widi/California_Fur_Rush

VI. Gold Spanish coins were found around Rancho Refugio.

See how those historic coins are replicated for games and treasure hunts today.

https://www.amazon.com/Metal-Pirate-CoinsDoubloons Realistic/dp/B0821QY292/ref=sr_1_6?dchild=1&keywords= spanish+pirate+coins&qid=1621720459&sr=8-6

VII. All the Pacific Coast ports and presidios made news.

Find their stories in the news and tall tales of California in the 1800s:

https://www.maritimeheritage.org/news/SF02081849.html

VIII. Shipping records in early California

The fictional port at Refugio is similar to many historic ports. The Maritime Heritage Project helps you investigate the real history of shipping in early California, including ships, cargo, captains, and old newspaper clippings.

https://www.maritimeheritage.org/news/SF02081849.html

IX. Alicia speaks to Masagawa on the beach near the ancestral shell mounds.

Learn the real history of shell mounds in California, as well as other Native American traditions throughout North America.

https://sites.coloradocollege.edu/indigenoustraditions/ sacred-lands/san-bruno-mountain-shellmound/

X. Papa told Alicia he saw many Americans exploring Texas and California.

See who those early explorers and frontiersmen were, and who they worked for, in the list, Legends of America:

https://www.legendsofamerica.com/explorer-list

Spanish Language Vocabulary List

On the first occurrence of Spanish words, they appear in italics; thereafter, in Roman type.

Chapter 1

hacienda	ranch, estate
refugio	refuge
cuidate	be careful
mija	my daughter
Chumash	Indigenous people groups of the SW north American continent
adobe	mud brick
sala	living room/parlor
familias	families
padre	father/priest

Chapter 2

cierto	sure/true

Chapter 3

veranda	covered front patio
manzanita	a native California evergreen
presidio	fort/garrison
savvy (saber)	to know

Chapter 4

fiesta	holiday/party
rancho	ranch

Chapter 5

pueblo	town/village
ramada	shelter/covering
molcajete	grinding stone

Chapter 7

Portolá	Gaspar de Portola, Spanish explorer (1716–1786)

Chapter 8

Pedro	Peter
Flaco	thin/skinny

Chapter 9

tomol boat	a plank-built Chumash boat

Chapter 10

mil gracias	many (one thousand) thanks

Chapter 11

bendiciones todos	blessings on everyone

Chapter 12

sí	yes
tío	uncle
Alta California	upper California
fuego	fire
hombres	men (plural)

Chapter 13

| Spanish galleon | Spanish warship; later trade ship, fifteenth–seventeenth centuries |
| a el oro de España | to the Spanish gold |

Chapter 14

con leche	with milk
pan tostado	toast
fresas con crema	strawberries with cream

Chapter 15

| loco | crazy/mad |

Chapter 17

| borracho | drunkard |

Chapter 18

| señora | misses/Mrs. |
| cinturón | belt |

Chapter 19

cálmate mijita	calm down my little girl
fíjate	imagine
pobrecito	poor little thing
regalitos	small gifts

Chapter 20

Cadiz	ancient port city in Andalucía region of SW Spain
la vida no vale nada	life is worthless
entrando cuando llorando	you come in cryin'

Chapter 21

rebozo	a long scarf
bienvenido	welcome
a sus ordenes	at your service
disculpe	excuse me
valise	suitcase
hola	hello
adiós	goodbye
buenas noches	goodnight

Chapter 22

siesta	midday nap

Chapter 23

tía	aunt
hermanos	brothers
cena	meal
adelante	hurry
comida	food
feliz cumpleaños	happy birthday
quinceañera	fifteenth birthday
señor	sir

Chapter 31

Provecho	to your health

Chapter 34

señorita	Miss
afuera	outside
Chata	[slang] a person with a small or snub nose
conmigo	with me

Chapter 41

bebidas	beverages
salud	health/cheers

Chapter 42

cantina	tavern/bar
padrino	godfather
la señora de la Guerra	Mrs. de la Guerra
comandante	commander

Chapter 45

puerto oficial	official port

Chapter 47

Carlitos	little Carlos

www.ingramcontent.com/pod-product-compliance
Lightning Source LLC
Chambersburg PA
CBHW020149120726
47903CB00007B/2478